ARE YOU SEEING ME?

ARE YOU SEEING ME?

DARREN GROTH

ORCA BOOK PUBLISHERS

TEEN

Library and Archives Canada Cataloguing in Publication

Groth, Darren, 1969–, author
Are you seeing me? / Darren Groth.

Originally published: North Sydney, NSW : Woolshed Press, an imprint
of Random House Australia, 2014.

Issued in print and electronic formats.
ISBN 978-1-4598-1079-2 (bound).—ISBN 978-1-4598-1080-8 (pdf).—
ISBN 978-1-4598-1081-5 (epub)

I. Title.
PS8613.R698A74 2015   jc813'.6   C2015-901548-0
C2015-901549-9

First published by Woolshed Press, 2014
First published in the United States, 2015
Library of Congress Control Number: 2015934240

Summary: In this novel, twins Justine and Perry have left their home in Australia
and embarked on the road trip of a lifetime in the Pacific Northwest.

FSC
MIX
Paper from
responsible sources
FSC® C016245
www.fsc.org

*Orca Book Publishers is dedicated to preserving the environment and has
printed this book on Forest Stewardship Council® certified paper.*

Orca Book Publishers gratefully acknowledges the support for its publishing
programs provided by the following agencies: the Government of Canada through
the Canada Book Fund and the Canada Council for the Arts, and the Province of British
Columbia through the BC Arts Council and the Book Publishing Tax Credit.

Cover images from Shutterstock.com: silhouettes © freesoulproduction, crack © farmer79,
tentacles © shockfactor.de, car © Jennifer Gottschalk, road sign © VoodooDot
Jacket design by Christabella Designs and Teresa Bubela
Author photo by Lauren White

ORCA BOOK PUBLISHERS
www.orcabook.com

Printed and bound in Canada.

18 17 16 15 • 4 3 2 1

For W, for J and especially for C

We are all dependent on one another,
every soul of us on earth.
GEORGE BERNARD SHAW

JUSTINE

PERRY IS STANDING ON THE far side of the metal detector, feet planted on the red stripe. Beads of sweat dot his forehead. His right leg twitches, keeping pace with some inaudible rhythm. At regular intervals, his lips curl inward then spring open, releasing a loud *pop*. He's stuck. He's been stuck for a while.

There'll be another announcement over the PA soon. I imagine it being a little more pointed than its predecessor: *Ms. Justine Richter, Mr. Perry Richter, you are required to board Flight 47 to Vancouver. Your fellow passengers are waiting for you to end this madness. Can you blame them for getting upset? I can't…What is your problem? Are you unaware of anyone but yourselves? You think the whole world should bow to your needs? The two of you are an absolute disgrace.*

I attempt to catch Perry's eye with reassuring nods and here-is-your-loving-sister hand gestures. I won't approach him or get in his face. I won't negotiate either— speeches are useless when my brother has reached this level of anxiety. It's like trying to draw attention to a lit candle during a laser show.

The stolid security officer holding the metal-detecting paddle displays a frown. "Please step through, sir," he says for the millionth time.

The sour business suit behind Perry huffs and places his hands on his hips. "No worries, pal," he says. "It's not like we've got planes to catch or anything."

Perry hears none of it. His hands are clasped together on top of his head. A pronounced lean has gripped the left side of his body. The *pops* have morphed into heavy sighs. The soles of his shoes remain fixed to the red stripe.

This is my nightmare. Sure, there are any number of planks in the rickety suspension bridge of our trip that could give out and send us plummeting—the flight, the hotels, the road trips to Okanagan Lake and Seattle. Foreign places, foreign people. Foreign *everything*. And, of course, The Appointment and all of the question marks it entails. But to go wrong here? *Here?* At the *airport?* On the list of places you'd want to avoid acting out of the ordinary, the airport would rank number one with a bullet. Or maybe a Taser.

I pull the rubber band at my wrist, let it snap back. The blossom of pain strangles the panic, rouses a resilience honed over the last two years. Perry needs help—it is right and just that I provide it. This is his time. His ultimate holiday. He deserves all the patience and tolerance required to make the next two weeks a memory for the ages.

I take a couple of steps forward and stand tall, framed by the metal detector. Like a mime playing to the back row, an exaggerated level of animation overtakes my movements. I nod my head until my neck hurts. I tap my watch with large stabbing points of the index finger. I wheel my arm over like an air guitarist in full flight. The performance makes a minor impression; Perry has returned to vertical, and the volume has been turned down on his sighs. I'm ready for a second dance of persuasion when a voice to my left interjects.

"He'll get there, miss."

I look toward the reassurer. It's the security officer seated by the X-ray machine. She's a cement block of a woman with dyed black hair and a red blotchy face. In contrast to her body, her expression is open, soft. The conveyor belt of luggage that is her charge has been halted. I hesitate, wary of reconciling compassion with authority, then nod.

"I've got a nephew like him. Similar age, by the look of it." She juts her chin and sits up a little straighter in her chair. "You're doin' real good."

Nephew or not, she has no real clue, but I mouth the words *thank you* anyway.

As I turn back toward the stalemate, she adds, "You take as much time as you need."

Her gracious sentiment is not a shared one. The paddle wielder has dropped the *sir* from his requests.

The suit barges back through the line in search of a security station that "doesn't have a goddamn retard holding everything up." A small part of me is proud of Pez for upending their crappy little ordered empires. The rest of me is still locked on his unraveling.

And then things go from bad to worse. Perry bends at the knees, buckling slowly, like Atlas defeated. The implications are immediate—if his knees hit the floor, it's a done deal. He'll go to all fours, then onto his stomach. Perhaps he'll roll over on his back. Whatever the final position, he'll be spread-eagled and staked. Ninety-one kilograms of dead weight destined for full-blown security intervention. The clock, previously at a premium, is seconds away from becoming redundant.

He's halfway down when an idea strikes. I lunge for the counter and unzip the bag Perry packed for the trip. I scrabble around among his essentials, assessing their candidacy. The seismometer? Too valuable. The DVD of Jackie Chan's *Drunken Master II*? Too fragile. The Ogopogo stuffed toy? Too childish. The CD of *Polka Hits from Around the World*?! Too…weird. The book *Quakeshake: A Child's Experience of the Newcastle Earthquake*?

Bingo!

I snatch up the book and hustle into position. I turn side-on, then cock my wrist, ready for the throw. It's all or nothing, anything but a gimme; the toss must negotiate the metal detector and land at Perry's feet. If it falls short, it will lack the impact to snap my brother out of his descent. If it sails long, it will hit him in the head, leading to a million YouTube hits. The task would test a decent athlete, let alone a generous-hipped, Cornetto-eating girl who turned excuse letters for PE class into an art form. I take an awkward practice swing, then eye the target. Perry is now down on his haunches, rocking on the balls of his feet. It's now or never. I draw back. A king tide of blood pummels my eardrums. The onlookers are panes of glass. Somewhere, in the distant burbs of my mind, I ask: *How did my job description become flinging books at my twin brother to avoid disaster?*

The throw clears the metal detector, hits the floor and skims a few meters before coming to rest at the toe of Perry's right shoe. For a fleeting moment, there is only stillness, the wait to discover if the tall ship of clarity has dropped anchor in the swirling eddies of sensory distress.

Perry grasps the book. He opens it, begins flipping through the pages. After a few seconds, he stands up. The flush in his face is retreating. His breaths are slowing.

He is present.

He is seeing me.

I bite my tongue. "Come through, Pez. It's okay."

The command is barely complete when my brother walks forward. He holds the book out as he enters the detector, clutches it to his chest as he emerges on the other side. No beeps or buzzes or red lights. I glance at Paddle Man—he looks disappointed. Perry heads for the counter and his carry-on suitcase. He shoves the book back in among his prized possessions and pulls the zipper closed.

"I'm sorry, Justine," he murmurs, fixing his gaze on the stack of empty plastic trays by his left elbow. "I was quite worried."

"No kidding. Don't you remember our talk this morning? We went over the detector stuff ten times. And we made sure you weren't wearing any metal."

He nods. "I remember. Those detectors don't work properly. I saw an article online. Sometimes they malfunction and make noise when they don't mean to. I didn't want to hear that noise. It would hurt my ears. And I imagined the security man touching my armpits and the front of my pants, then yelling at me and throwing me to the ground. He thought I was a terrorist—"

"Okay, okay. It's done now."

"I couldn't help it. I'm sorry, Justine."

"Yeah, I know you are."

I grab my bag and sling it over my shoulder. I'm about to lay bare the supreme urgency of our situation when

Perry takes my hand. He secures only the middle, ring and pinkie fingers. It is a recognizable and comforting contact. He first held my hand this way in third grade. I can't recall him ever holding my hand differently.

"Because we are late, I think it is logical we run to gate twenty-six."

I scoff. "I like that—*we* are late."

He tugs me along for a few meters, then releases. In a flash, he is past the duty-free shop and on the moving walkway, suitcase of consolations by his side. I set off after him, ignoring the leftover tremors in my legs and the visions of rickety suspension bridges in my head.

...........●●●...........

WHEN I FLOP DOWN INTO my aisle seat on Flight 47 to Vancouver, it's a victory. We've made it this far. There is a journey to come—starting with fifteen hours nonstop across the Pacific—but this is a moment to savor. I want to ask the nearest hostess to give three cheers during the safety demonstration.

Perry is across from me. It was my plan to have the two of us sit together but apart, each with easy access to the aisle. It was also important that Perry be seated beside an adult. An early-morning need for a toilet or an attendant's help could be a tad disruptive to a sleeping child. Not nearly as unsettling as a shouted quote from *Shanghai Noon* or an impromptu rendition of "Born This Way." Though, if one of those meteorites fell from the sky…well, we'd all just have to wait until it burned out. Hopefully, the damage would be minimal. Firefighter Jus would, of course, be on hand with a bucket and a garden hose.

An announcement from the captain assures us we'll be taxiing out to the runway in ten to fifteen minutes. There's been a delay in the fueling procedure. I study Perry's reaction to the news. He shifts in his seat and squeezes his hands together hard, causing the knuckles to blanch. He takes two long breaths. The passengers alongside him—husband and wife, late fifties, holding the morning edition of *The Australian* and a Kimberley Freeman novel—give Perry an obvious, but not unkind, once-over.

"Afraid of flying, mate?" the husband asks.

Perry directs his gaze at the armrest between them. He inches over in his seat, closer to the aisle. Closer to me. He shakes his head. "I like jets."

"Yeah?"

"Yes, I do."

"Oh, okay. Just thought you looked a bit nervous."

Perry does like planes. He has several model bombers he built from kits. And he bought a replica Qantas jet from Myer the day I told him we had tickets to North America. Actual flying? No idea. This is his first ride in a big bird.

The man smiles and offers his hand. "I'm Ross, by the way."

Perry accepts, pumps three times, withdraws. His eyes move from the armrest to Ross's secured tray table. "My name is Perry Richter. I'm very pleased to meet you."

"Good to meet you, Perry. This is my wife, Jane."

"Good to meet you, Ross. Good to meet you, Jane."

There's a pause. Ross taps his chin twice, narrows his eyes. I recognize the signs. He's had his first inkling that the young guy in seat 39G is not fashioned from a familiar mold. Bravo, Ross! Unless the association is patently obvious—Perry's under stress or immersed in one of his favorite obsessions—it takes most people a while to suspect my brother is a bit skewiff. It's one of his weightier burdens: look like everyone else, act like no one you've ever seen.

It's also the main reason I'm up front about it. Before people get confused or angry or frustrated or gooey or freaked out, I give them the standard spiel: *Perry has a brain condition that can cause him to feel anxious or upset in different places and circumstances. He has trouble with people—mixing with them and communicating with them—and it sometimes results in*

11

inappropriate behaviors. I appreciate your understanding and patience.

Depending on my own reserves of patience, I might embellish it from time to time:

What the hell are you staring at?

Why don't you take a picture? It lasts longer.

If the wind changes, you'll look like that permanently.

You've never seen a disabled person and their homicidal caregiver before?

At these times, I know for sure I am my father's daughter. He never sought to explain Perry to the public. *Let 'em get an education,* he would say. *If they don't want to be educated, they can go jump.*

I lean in as Ross's education commences.

"Did you know that the earth is made up of four layers?" asks Perry. "There's the core—actually *two* cores: inner and outer—and the mantle and the crust. The crust is where we live. No lie. I like the mantle the best out of the four. It's mainly made up of molten lava, and the crust floats on top of it and is always moving. Isn't that *cool*?"

Ross glances left and right, then nods.

"That's a funny joke, saying it's cool, because the temperature can actually rise to 5,400 degrees Celsius. Anyway, scientists call the moving *convection*. They also have a theory that we are living on a series of tectonic plates floating on the mantle. Some say twelve, others say it's more than twelve. I'm not sure who is correct. One thing is certain, though—the plates can rub together or pull away from each other or smash into each other or one might go underneath the other. These events are what cause earthquakes to occur, and of course earthquakes are measured on the moment magnitude scale, but they used to be measured on the Richter scale. That's my last name—Richter. No lie. My father used to say it was *my* scale and that was a funny joke too, because it was invented by Charles Richter in 1935, which is fifty-five years before I was born. In fact, it was twenty-eight years before my father was born—"

"Uh, Pez?"

Perry halts his runaway train of thought, takes a breath and begins lightly tapping the tips of his fingers together. He looks down at his seat-belt buckle. The couple stare in my direction.

"My name's Justine Richter. I'm Perry's sister and caregiver. Just so you know, Perry has a brain condition. It can cause him to feel—"

"Brain condition?" asks Jane.

"Yes. That's right."

"So, is he one of those people who are very good with numbers?"

"I *am* good with numbers," confirms Perry.

The husband arches his brow and twists in his seat. "What's 1,491 times 6,218?"

Perry thinks for a second, then unbuckles his seat belt, leaps out of his chair and opens the overhead bin. Ross stares at me, eyebrows high on his forehead.

"It's coming," I say. "Takes him a little longer than the ones they trot out on TV."

Perry closes the compartment and flops back down in his chair. He's holding a calculator. "What were those numbers again, Ross?"

"I...I can't remember."

"Was it 1,491 times 6,218? Or was it 4,191 times 2,618?"

"I...I don't know."

"Let's try the first one." Perry brings the calculator up very close to his chin and punches in the equation, emphasizing each digit entry with a small nod. When the sum is done, he thrusts the calculator at Ross's face, causing him to rear back. "Is this the correct answer, Ross?"

"I've got no idea."

"Oh. I thought you knew the answer."

"You took the words out of my mouth, son."

Perry wrestles with the meaning of this for a moment. He twists his lips this way and that, voices a quiet hum, then gives up. He stashes the calculator in the seat pocket, then starts playing with his touchscreen video monitor. I'm ready to provide some assistance, but he doesn't need it. Within seconds he's wearing earbuds and watching the opening sequences of a documentary on saltwater crocodiles.

I engage the couple with a clipped smile. "Perry has trouble with people—mixing with them and communicating with them—and it sometimes results in inappropriate behaviors. I appreciate your understanding and patience."

"Reckon I might've been the one with the inappropriate behaviors, love," says Ross.

"Make that two of us," adds Jane.

I study their earnest faces. No need for further education here. Class is dismissed. "It's fine," I say. "All good."

They breathe a sigh of relief. Jane asks Ross to sit back so she can see me. "Thank you," she says. "It's Justine, isn't it?"

"That's right."

"Justine, if you don't mind me asking, did you say you were Perry's sister *and* caregiver?"

"Yes."

"Do you mean just for your trip?"

"No, I'm his sister all the time." A *badum-tish* follows. I announce that I'm here all week and ask that they don't forget to tip the waitress. Jane blinks three times. "Sorry, my jokes aren't as good as Perry's. The answer to your question is no, I am the current full-time caregiver for my brother."

Jane places a hand on her breast and tilts her head. "Oh, that must be so difficult for you."

"Ow! That's gotta hurt!" Perry mimics a crocodile's lunge and snap with his hand. His focus remains on the small screen.

"It has its moments," I reply.

"Wow. You must be an amazing person to do that, especially on your own. Do you have any help at all?"

The question loiters in the aisle like abandoned luggage. Then it's in my lap, heavy and pointed. I'm overtaken by a desire to share it all with these people, these complete and decent strangers. To tell them how our mother left and we were raised by our father. How he did the best he could, better than he was obliged to do. Then he up and died two weeks shy of our eighteenth birthdays. And even though he swore on his deathbed I was ready—that my future was more than just being my brother's keeper—the two years following made his words seem like a coin tossed into a wishing well.

Do I have any help? It's coming. When this holiday is over and we touch down again in Brisbane Town, the balance my father wanted will be possible. "Home" will be elsewhere for Perry. "Dependence" will be measured by degrees. The wishing well will answer with the name Fair Go Community Village. Yes, help is coming, all right.

But the truth is, I never asked for it.

I want to tell these polite outsiders all of this and assure them of one last, important fact: I am *not* an amazing person. But the itch to unburden recedes when we're interrupted by the pilot's update. "Apologies, again, for the delay, folks. We are all set to go now. Shouldn't be a problem making up for lost time."

I shift my attention from Jane to Perry. He senses the rolling movement of the plane and removes his earbuds.

"We're moving," he announces. He digs around in the seat pocket and extracts the laminated safety card. He lifts it high so it is visible to the passengers behind him. "If we crash on takeoff, I can help save some of you! No lie, I have first-aid expertise!"

"Shoosh!" I rein Perry in with a tug on his forearm. Amid the crowd murmurings—some good-natured, others not so forgiving—I turn back to Jane. "Why would I need any help?"

................●●●.............

2:12 AM, VANCOUVER TIME. The lights in the cabin have been dimmed and economy class is in various states of slumber. The burring jet engines are occasionally punctuated by a chunky snore or a muffled cough or a baby's cry.

I lean over to check on Perry. He's out. Head tilting right and forward, his eyelids flutter. The small, orb-shaped seismometer is cradled in his lap like a snuggling pet. His seat is bolt upright. My desire to press the armrest button and ease him back into a more reclined position pales next to the prospect of waking him up. He's done well so far—he's earned some uninterrupted rest. Hell, so have I.

"Worn out" doesn't begin to describe my exhaustion. I rub my eyes until there are raw tears. Sleep won't come for a while yet. The uncomfortable seat is partially guilty, but Perry's the main culprit. Perry and the dark. For years as a child, I thought the nighttime knew secrets about my brother, that if I was close enough and awake enough, those secrets would be revealed in a sign or a vision or a whisper. Maybe I would learn the cause of his condition? A body toxin unidentified at birth. Some faulty genetic code spelled out in terms a science-shunning, literature-loving girl could understand. Maybe I'd be given the solution to his riddle? The power to bestow upon him all the unspoken language skills the rest of us take for granted? Or perhaps I'd be "made" like him for a few predawn hours; all the traits would be mine: the twitches, the ticks, the routines and the obsessions. I would think too fast and feel too much. I would try to be the same as everyone else in this world, and I would set the frustration and the anger and the despair free when it proved impossible. Then I would be Justine again, only new and improved, knowing my brother's existence completely, working to bring about greater understanding in the "normal" world.

With those nocturnal revelations so tantalizingly close, deferring sleep became a habit when Perry was in the same space. It took hold when we were little kids, and was reinforced when we went camping or on holidays.

It came back in a big way after Dad died.

I need Dad now. I reach down and reef the bag out from under the seat in front. Amongst the contents is the weathered hardback I can identify by touch and smell alone. Red and purple roses on the cover. Faded, felt-pen title in block letters. *The Life and Times of a Tree Frog*— the journal my father faithfully kept for seventeen years and fifty weeks. I open it to page one and listen for his voice: a gentle and unhurried baritone, nothing like the wispy croak he had in his final days.

·········●●●·········

21 October 1990

Hello, Justine. If you're reading this, it's 21 October 2008 and you've just turned eighteen. Happy Birthday! I wanted to do something special for the two of you, starting on the day you were born. Well, that's today. Mum gave birth to you this morning—you first at 11:26, Perry three minutes later—and this is the special something. A journal. One for you and one for your brother. Eighteen years in the making. I hope you like it.

Originally, I thought about doing some videos. Not like regular home movies of our holidays or Christmases. More personal ones, with stories and memories. Ones you could look back at and say, "That's my dad, all right!" But I figured it would be difficult keeping it a secret when you guys were older. And all those tapes! How would I know if you had a Betamax recorder when you became an adult?

No, I decided I should do something different. A challenge. Something that needed a real commitment. Something I would never do for myself and something that I would only ever do for my two minnows (twinnows!).

I'm not much of a writer, but a journal seemed like a good idea...

·············●············

29 October 1990

We've been home a few days and it's bloody busy! Even though we're flat out, my mind keeps going back to our first moment together. You were so beautiful when you came into the world. The doc lifted you out of your mother's belly, the nurse wrapped you up…then you were in my arms. You were tiny, just under five pounds. Not bad for a preemie arriving six weeks early. You looked right at me with those big, dark eyes. It was as if you knew exactly who I was and what I was feeling inside.

Your brother's exit wasn't as smooth. I don't think he knew what had hit him when he was taken out. He didn't breathe straight away, but he got it done when he had to. A part of me likes to think he did it on purpose so he could get a little extra care and attention from those good sorts of nurses. He went to Mum first. She had trouble holding him because she was drugged to the eyeballs, so they handed him over to me. He didn't open his eyes the way you did. He stayed asleep, as if the rest of the world didn't matter.

..........●..........

4 May 1991

You've started doing something that gives me a good laugh. When you're eating the apple mush that you seem to like better than anything else on the mush menu, you gulp a mouthful down and then poke your tongue out. Every time! Mum says it's gross. I think it's bloody brilliant! Like a green tree frog catching flies!

Your brother doesn't perform this little gem, but he's got his own comedy going on. The witchlike cackle. The backstroke attempts in the bath. The projectile pee—one of which ended up hosing the neighbor's cat as it was having a stickybeak on the windowsill. I almost couldn't breathe I laughed so hard!

It's nice to have a few howlers here and there. Now that I'm back at the factory, Mum's on her own all day. She gets exhausted. Things would be much better if getting Perry to sleep—day or night—hadn't been a real struggle the last month. Lots of tears and screams and not a lot of zees. Mum wants to let him cry it out, but I'm not keen. I don't think it's right. I mean, he's crying for a reason, isn't he? Probably the teeth coming through. I reckon once he's over the worst of it, he'll sleep like, well, a baby.

In the meantime, I've got my little tree frog to keep me entertained.

...........●●●...........

15 July 1991

Holy bloody hell! You just walked! You pulled yourself up onto your feet with the help of the coffee table, took one hand away, took the other hand away, and toddled across the living room! Wow! So proud of you!

Hopefully you can relive the moment when Mum gets back. I had a feeling she would miss a one-off like this. She's been going out quite a bit lately, getting her "mental health time," as she likes to call it.

Perry saw you walk. He was over by the azaleas, mucking around with his Cookie Monster cushion. When you got up, he stopped and turned his attention to you. He watched you all the way, until you plopped back down on your bum near the bookshelf. Then he made a noise and held his arms up, like he was cheering for you! Okay, maybe he wasn't cheering, but he certainly took notice of your great work. Hope he took a few notes—he's still motoring around the house on his knees. The books say it's not uncommon for boys to reach milestones later than girls.

He is saying a few words though: "dog" and "Dad" and "fan," so that's good. He'll be all right, especially with his big sister showing the way.

...............●...............

20 November 1991

I might have had too many hits on the hard hat, but it seems to me Perry's gone backward a bit of late. He's doing some funny things with his toys. He'll put his Tonka trucks all in a row and stare at them from this angle and that. Then he'll turn them upside down and spin their wheels, over and over and over again. Also, he's not saying the words he was saying a couple of months ago. And he won't look at you anymore when you say his name. I wondered for a while if he might be deaf, but he never seemed to have any problems hearing a packet of gingersnaps being opened. Anyway, we got his ears checked and there were no problems.

Mum and I took him back to the clinic on Saturday (Grandma took care of you; she said, as per usual, you were an angel). Early on, the doc mentioned that it could be some sort of brain issue. She said it was too early to tell. Then she thought for a bit longer and shook her head.

She said Perry having problems long-term was pretty unlikely and she wouldn't want to put a label on him when, in all likelihood, he was just delayed in his development. After a time, some of these behaviors would go away and we'd see him start to catch up. Mum shook her hand like Robinson Crusoe meeting the captain of the rescue boat. In the car going home, she told me she'd known all along our boy was just a bit slow, and her job was tough enough without a husband getting worried for nothing. I'm not convinced.

I'm sorry I'm going on about Perry so much—this stuff should go into his journal, I suppose. I'm not writing in his book these days. It was just dribs and drabs for a while, but now I've stopped altogether. It seems unfair to be recording his moments right now when he's standing still and you're zooming ahead. But that doesn't mean this journal should be filled with your brother's troubles and your father's worries.

This is your gift, your memories to look back on.

···········●···········

RETURNING DAD'S JOURNAL TO THE BAG, I find my phone jammed into the pages of my current read: a dog-eared, secondhand paperback of *Robinson Crusoe*. I extract the phone and begin scrolling through Marc's messages. I linger on the most recent one:

> **Hope u made it through security ok. Have a gr8 trip. Can't wait until u come back.**
>
> **xo**

"Can't wait"—that phrase sums him up. Point blank and a perfect stranger, he asked me out for coffee in Woolies (frozen section, to be exact). I noted his basket contained a few favorites from my food pyramid: Tim Tams, Mount Franklin water, a ripe mango. His look had some favorites too. Blue eyes. Cropped beard. Soft, wistful face that hinted at James McAvoy in *Becoming Jane*. Long eyelashes.

"I have a brother at home and it's just the two of us," I told him. "His name is Perry. He has a brain condition that can cause him to feel anxious or upset in different places and circumstances. He has trouble with people— mixing with them and communicating with them—and it sometimes results in inappropriate behaviors. Still want to have coffee?"

"More than ever," he replied.

I agreed to meet up.

We sipped espressos and split a Devonshire tea at Riverbend Books in Bulimba, and the discussion of which novels should never have been made into films went well enough to pencil in a second coffee date. He got down on one knee and proposed during that one. When I rejected him, laughing loud enough to disturb other tables, he told me he wasn't serious. I suspect it was a half-truth.

We got to know each other a bit better over the next month—three dinners, two Sunday brunches, one movie (*Black Swan*—it was a tad awkward) and one sleepover at his shared house in New Farm. In February, he admitted he could see us living together sometime very soon. The time had arrived to properly introduce Master Disaster. I got down on one knee and proposed Marc join us for a barbecue at Chez Richter.

They went okay. Perry was quiet, not his usual talkative self. Marc tried hard, probably too hard. It was obvious a few of my brother's chestnuts had him scrambling for rationales. When the hang-out was over, Marc reassured me I needn't worry. He and Pez would be best mates before long. And future living arrangements? Those things would sort themselves out "in the fullness of time." Six months on, Time is not merely full, it is fit to burst.

Marc told me at the departure gate he'd be fine if the plan changed after the trip; if I were to come back second-guessing Perry's move out of home, he wouldn't be averse to living with us if that was the easiest way forward.

In the moment, the revelation seemed a bit desperate—arrhythmic beats of a heart-on-the-sleeve already feeling the squeeze of separation. But looking back on it now, I think Marc meant what he said. Sweet gesture, for sure. And totally unnecessary.

It's not that Marc and Perry couldn't handle the arrangement; Marc's best-mates promise may not have been fulfilled, but a distance has been traveled. A small though solid foundation of shared experience now exists between them—bodysurfing at Rainbow Beach, pancake breakfasts, car washes, Mario Kart. Marc's surprising knowledge and appreciation of Jackie Chan movies hasn't hurt either. And a four-day camping trip to Girraween in June showed me the two of them were comfortable—with a small *c*—in close quarters.

No, it's simply this: there isn't going to be any back-tracking on a decision already made. Two weeks on the other side of the world doesn't alter the reality at home: Perry wants to move out, period. My wish for him to stay is just selfishness on my part, and I would never deny him what he truly desires. Not when the rest of "normal" society denies him so much already. And maybe he *needs* to move out. He can handle life at a supported residence. He is capable. More people, other people, *nice* people—not just his loving but imperfect twin—they can only be good for him.

Marc and his sweet gestures are still new to all this. A white knight riding in on his valiant steed is not what we need.

My final rummage through the bag is for the manila folder labeled *Perry's New Adventure*. It contains a host of documents—maps, pictures, lists of services, resident testimonials. I lift a page from the pile: *Fair Go Community Village—Where Special Needs and Life Purpose Come Together.* A crisp, glossy flyer once upon a time, it's now crumpled and stained. I know its content well. Regardless, I skim through the various sections, starting with "Our Mission for a Fair Go" and ending with "Contact Us Today—The Vision is Now!"

For the thousandth time, I try to trace the timeline in my head, but it remains elusive. I put the starting date in the initial weeks—perhaps days—after Dad's diagnosis. Finding a safety net for his son once it was clear he himself was in free fall? Makes sense. Dad was nothing if not a realist. Over the month following, there must have been phone calls, emails. I remember he went out for a drive one day even though he looked like death warmed over. He got back around seven in the evening and refused to tell us where he'd been, despite my best efforts to get it out of him. Given Fair Go's location— about an hour's drive northwest of the Brisbane central business district—it's reasonable to assume he spent the day there. A week or two later, maybe six weeks in total after the initial inquiry, Perry was assigned to the residential waiting list. If Dad was provided with documentation confirming this fact, I've never seen it.

Why did you never mention it to me, Dad? Or write it in *Tree Frog*? Taking this decision to the grave, relying on a reminder in the mail twelve months later—was that fair? Leaving the final follow-through in the hands of a kid—was that a good idea? And hear the truth, Dad: I *am* a kid. You always saw me as mature. You called me an "old soul" and "wise beyond my years." I craved that praise. Making you proud—it allowed everything to be manageable, reasonable. But it couldn't mask the truth: I was a kid. And then you went and bloody died, didn't you? You took my sustenance away before I could grow up big and strong. No praise. No nourishing words. Just echoes in a journal and a document in the mail and a responsibility far too colossal for a make-believe adult.

I'll never know what drove Dad to conceal it. What I do know is the sequence that followed. I showed Perry the form, explained what it meant as best I could and why it had come into our lives. I assured him it was totally his call to stay or go.

He thought about it for three days.

I cried.

Perry told me he wanted to go.

I cried some more.

Perry said I shouldn't cry because living away from your twin wasn't nearly as difficult as being the sole survivor of an earthquake.

Sleep is finally at hand. In keeping with tradition, the nighttime has offered hours of contemplation but no epiphany. I consider reading a few paragraphs of *Robinson Crusoe,* then reject the idea. Slaves, shipwrecks, cannibals, mutineers…Defoe's tale was not designed to bring about rest. I check that the seat is as far back as the button will allow and pull the thin blanket up to my chin.

The last thing I am aware of before the black curtain falls is Perry's position. He's pivoted on his right shoulder so he's facing me. I think he's peeking through half-closed eyes.

·············●●●·············

A DREAM. I KNOW THIS is a dream. That's as far as my powers extend; I can't influence what's happening or call a halt to the scene. Just have to ride along with it, see where it takes me.

I'm aboard a small boat. Land is near. There are palms and ferns and trees laden with coconuts. It's not anywhere I've been in Australia. I'm certain it's not any of our North American stops.

I drop anchor a short swim from shore, but I stay seated. There is a primal crook of fear tugging at me in unison with the prevailing south wind. I look down at my hands. They're shaking. And they belong to a stranger. Patches of dark, coarse hair gather above the wrists and between the knuckles. The fingernails are cracked and caked with salt. Blisters and burns wrack the skin. I stare at them until a monstrous roar from the island thrusts me back into the moment.

"I don't like that."

My companion has spoken. The voice is unmistakably Perry's; so, too, is the rocking from side to side and finger flicking. The body, though, belongs to a boy, weathered and sinewy. A lightbulb flares overhead. This is Defoe's vision. Perry is Xury. I am Crusoe. This is the island landing scene following the castaways' escape from the Moors. A warped hallucination of the scene, no doubt.

"I don't like that," repeats Perry/Xury. "But I have to go."

"You *have* to?"

"Yes, Just Jeans. No lie, I have to."

"Why?"

"Because we can't survive like this. We won't make it."

Another bellow thunders out of the island brush. Perry/Xury cups his ears until the echoes die. The color of the river is changing, from a soft turquoise to a rich, almost royal, blue. The tropical, brackish air is cooling.

"Then we'll go together," I say.

Perry/Xury refuses, the way my brother is inclined to do when confronted with Mexican food or a slow Internet connection or someone else's equipment at the car wash: with great, sweeping head shakes. Before I can protest further, he pitches himself overboard. The water swallows him whole, with barely a ripple or a bubble.

I shout his name. Instinct demands I dive in after him. I try to stand and discover it's impossible. My body is made of brick, backside fastened to the seat with invisible mortar. I am Crusoe and I am enslaved again. Abandoned. I howl for Perry once more, and the reverberations awaken a frightening force on the island. A rumble from the depths of the earth rocks the landscape. Trees shake and fall. Great chunks of rock plunge down the mountainous backdrop. The river darkens to an oily black.

And as the world begins to tear at the seams, a voice penetrates the chaos. "We're close now. We're almost there…"

I think it belongs to my father.

·············●●●············

"WE'RE CLOSE NOW. WE'RE ALMOST THERE. We are only 632 kilometers from Vancouver."

I blink several times, find a grainy focus. Perry is leaning over me, his stubbly face centimeters from mine. His eyes are wide. His smile is ample. His breath is awful.

"You're awake now?"

"Yes, yes. I'm awake," I say, waving a hand in front of my face.

"You were making noises while you were sleeping."

"Was I?"

"Yes. You were."

I nudge Perry's shoulder and jab a thumb in the direction of his seat. He takes the hint.

"One time," he continues, "I had a dream I was inside an egg. Another time, I dreamed there was a springboard at Newmarket pool and I dived off it for a whole day, like Jackie Chan doing his famous hovercraft leap. I liked those dreams. Did you like your dream, Justine?"

"It was…interesting."

"Good." He squeezes one of his earbuds and stares at the compartment above my head. "I imagine I will dream about our trip to North America when I am back home. Actually, I think it is likely I will dream about our trip for the rest of my life."

He stamps the assertion with a single, purposeful nod and replaces his earbuds. Every few seconds, he quietly announces the kilometers remaining to destination: "Four hundred and ninety-four…487…481…"

I turn away and look out the nearest window. The Pacific Ocean below is vast and open and untroubled.

I hope it is prophetic of the dreams to come.

·············●●●············

DESPITE BEING THE LAST PAIR off the plane—Perry needed to do several head counts of his stuff before disembarking—our passage through the terminal is smooth and incident-free. We've barely settled in at the back of the long queue at Customs when an attendant directs us toward a newly opened station. I note the others granted special treatment: families, small- to medium-sized children. My overtired mind doesn't question the anomaly or argue blind luck. Of course we're special. We're about as special as they come.

Arriving at the security booth, I'm entertaining further five-star treatment: *Yes, go straight through. No need for passports. We love Australians here in Canada…We know you've had a rough flight. We know you've had a rough life. All those sharks and snakes and rugby players trying to kill you every moment of the day. Far be it from us to make things more difficult. And here, have this leftover gold medal from the Vancouver Winter Olympics. You've earned it.*

The Customs officer—Alan Hinton, according to his badge—doesn't think we're special. He has severe features and a bald head that is deeply sun-tanned. His expression is a dismal tableau of apathy and distrust.

"You mind telling me what he's doing, ma'am?"

One glance at Perry snaps me back to reality. He's lifted the entire earthquake kit from his carry-on. The seismometer is sitting dutifully by his feet. The portable seismograph, replete with buttons and plugs and tiny screen, occupies his right hand. A well-worn notepad is tucked under his left arm.

"Interesting," Perry says, studying the data. "Not much activity for a region with major fault zones."

I tell Officer Hinton that all is good and that normal service will be resumed as soon as possible, then give Perry his compliance orders: ten seconds or the kit is gone for the rest of the day. My brother swings into action, piling the equipment back into his suitcase. When the cleanup is complete, he stands to attention like a general. Striving for a tone that's offhand rather than anxious, I give Officer Hinton some bullet points of explanation:

It's earthquake-monitoring equipment.

My brother's obsessed with earthquakes.

He doesn't really use the equipment.

He has a brain condition.

Officer Hinton gives a shake of the head. It's a "Now I've seen it all" sort of gesture. He hands our documents back and barks for the next people in line to step forward. I mumble a thank-you and hustle Perry through. As my brother passes by the glass panel of the station, he waves to Officer Hinton. There is no acknowledgment in return.

The wait for our checked bags is mercifully short; it is just past 8 AM Vancouver time when we exit through the automatic doors and out into a mild, gray Sunday that, like its newest observers, appears sluggish and unsure of itself. I suggest a photo to record the moment. Perry is typically guarded—"The flash makes my eyes go funny"—but he doesn't refuse. I pull him close, lean in, cheek to cheek, and hold my phone above our heads. "Say cheese."

"Gorgonzola!"

The result is less than stellar.

"Try again," I say, tightening my hold on his shoulder. "Say cheese!"

"Just Jeans!"

Second time around, the snap is more than money— it is perfect. Our eyes are ablaze. Our grins are starlight.

Despite the fifteen-hour flight and lack of sleep, we have been captured at some sort of fission point, the release permitting the very best of our past, present and future to burst through for a nanosecond. As I stand there, spellbound, breathing the gluggy Vancouver air, the photograph materializes in other places, other times.

On my bedside table, keeping watch over a stack of my literary staples: Camus, de Beauvoir, the Brontës, Calvino, Thea Astley, Kate Morton…

Pinned to a corkboard on a wall painted in the Fair Go colors of Queensland maroon and wattle-tree gold…

In a Facebook album, likes and comments in the hundreds…

On an altar, flanked by our father's urn and a condolence registry…

The images fade as Perry eagerly points at the taxi stand. The cabbie at the head of the queue leans against the driver's door, smoking a thin cigar. When he spies our approach, he holds the cigar at arm's length, unsure of its disposal. For a brief moment, he considers his breast pocket. He decides against it. We're almost at his side when he sighs and drops it on the ground, mashes it into the pavement.

"Let me get those, miss," he says, pointing at the suitcases and waving the residual smoke away.

He's an older man, mid-to-late fifties, sporting a neatly trimmed goatee and glasses. His voice is quiet and his accent is undulating. I offer up the bags, state our destination—the Pacifica West Hotel at Canada Place—and tell Perry to hop in the back. He balks at first.

"Are you going to sit in the front seat, Just Jeans?"

"No, bud."

"Good. It's not rude to leave the front seat vacant, is it?"

"It's okay in a cab. And a limo."

"Which one is this?"

"This is a rickshaw."

He snorts, takes hold of my hand—middle finger to pinkie—and we climb in together.

In the first few minutes of the drive I soak up the wonder of a landscape demeaned by Google images and *Getaway* segments. The mountains are breathtaking. A gang of peaks—green, without a trace of winter white—stand to the north, jostling each other for the best view of the downtown metropolis. To the southeast, a snow-covered colossus, its girth partially obscured by a band of cloud, marks the horizon with an indelible stamp. The grass is emerald, no brown patches or dead streaks. The foliage on the trees is dense and rich. The peeking-through sun is a paler, more genial version of the Brisbane master I am used to. For every natural nuance I catch, Perry has a dozen more of the man-made variety. The North American names and symbols on the cars.

The severe, angled roofs of houses. Bundles of logs in the river. Buses attached to overhead electric wires. The occasional but prominent Canadian flags on shopfronts and billboards and bumper stickers. I feel a temporary stay of exhaustion: it is good to see such acute and complete distinction from the cityscape we know.

"You come from the Land Down Under, eh?"

I clear my throat. "Yes, we do. Picked it in one. You could tell we weren't from South Africa? Or New Zealand?"

"Or Japan!" cries Perry. "That's a funny joke, by the way."

The cabbie chuckles and nods. "Good one!" He spies me in the rearview mirror. "I've gotten pretty good at telling you folks apart, especially seeing as there's so many Aussies here. In Whistler, for sure. And Tofino." He holds his hand up. "My name's Jim. Jim Graydon. I like to introduce myself when there's international folks sharing a ride."

"Justine Richter."

"And my name is Perry Richter. I'm very pleased to meet you."

The left side of Jim's face crumples. "Ooh, Richter. That's a name that still hurts in this town. I don't know if you know, hockey is superclose to being religion here—"

"Ice hockey," clarifies Perry.

"Yes, *ice* hockey. We got a trophy called the Stanley Cup. All the teams in the National Hockey League play for it. Our team—"

"The Vancouver Canucks," asserts Perry.

"That's right. The 'Nucks made it to the finals of Lord Stanley back in 1994. Lost to the New York Rangers. Broke our hearts."

"I read somewhere there were riots afterward, yes?" I ask.

Jim nods. "I wasn't driving a cab back then. Glad of that." He points to a small mascot he has hanging from the rearview mirror. "Olympics this year showed we've grown up a lot. None too soon, I might add."

"Did a man called Richter start the riots?" asks Perry. "Is that why the name still hurts in these parts?"

Jim laughs. "No, the Rangers had a guy called Mike Richter in goal. He was good. Too good."

"The man who invented the Richter scale in 1935 was Charles Richter. That's fifty-five years before I was born."

Jim's mouth purses for a few seconds; then he shrugs. "I don't think this town has any argument with Charles Richter, young man."

"He's dead."

"We'll forgive him for that."

"My dad's dead too."

The levity falls off Jim's face like a poorly attached prosthetic. It's time to step in.

"Uh, Jim, my brother has a brain condition that can cause him to feel anxious or upset in different places and circumstances. He has trouble with people—mixing with them and communicating with them—and it sometimes—"

"Hold that thought." Jim digs around in his khakis, pulls out a small card and passes it back through the gap in the front seats. I immediately recognize the graphic—the ubiquitous single blue jigsaw piece. I read the text. It's a reasonable facsimile of my rote spiel.

"My boy—he'll be eleven in November. Third kid, only one from my second marriage. I was forty-four when he was born. Crazy, eh? Never thought I'd be a father again at that age. Never thought I'd be a 'special' dad either."

His hand trembles slightly as he takes the card back and tosses it onto the dash. He jiggles his head and pulls his shoulders back. Outside, a pale, wizened theater—the Metro, according to the sign—slides by on the left. It says three more chances remain to see Agatha Christie's *The Unexpected Guest.*

"My boy loves hockey, especially goaltenders," Jim continues. "He likes the equipment. I got him the full outfit, pads an' skates an' all. He doesn't play, just wears all the gear. And he loves the different painted masks the pros wear. It's kinda nice he's into goalies, 'cause two of 'em set up a support group for kids like him. Olaf Kölzig—used to be between the pipes for the Caps—he was one. Byron Dafoe—I think he was the other one."

"Defoe?" I ask.

"Yup."

"His name is Defoe?"

"I think it's spelled with an *a*...*Dah*-foe. They've raised a lot of money. Got a lot of other sportspeople involved."

Jim pauses, allowing a thoughtful silence. A bookshop called Characters catches my eye among the boxy procession of mom-and-pop stores. I smile. Sums up this taxi to a tee. On cue, Perry pokes me in the shoulder and indicates, via a series of facial contortions, that I should look out his window. The bus traveling alongside displays advertising for the Pacifica West Hotel. Every image, every loop and embellishment of the copy's font, communicates luxury.

"That's our first stop, isn't it, Justine?" he whispers.

"Yeah."

"And wealthy people go there, yes?"

"I reckon they probably do, yes."

I wait for an additional poser. It doesn't come. Perry hums a tune from one of his video games and resumes the role of spectator. I'm glad. The question of where the money came from for this trip has a simple answer:

Dad's life insurance. The slew of inquiries from Perry that would inevitably follow? *What's life insurance? How do they work it out? Is it like a lottery draw? Is there death insurance?* Not so simple to address those.

We cruise through intersections both chronological (41st, 33rd, 28th) and colonial (King Edward, Balfour, Angus). Properties with giant ramparts of hedge offer a brief glimpse into a world of money made beyond life-insurance payouts, courtesy of the driveway gates. A critical mass of unfamiliar banks and Asian restaurants and specialty shops with *Barn* in the title kicks in at 16th Avenue and carries through to the waterfront.

As we motor across the Granville Street Bridge, Perry leans into the middle of the passenger space and peers through the windshield. High-rises abound. He claps his hands. "Could we view the Qube building?"

"The what building, Pez?" I ask.

"The Qube building. *Q-U-B-E*, not *C-U-B-E*. It's a different spelling."

Jim whistles in approval. "You done some research about this town, eh?"

Perry nods. "The Qube was built especially to be earthquake-proof. It has a large concrete post in the center, and the building hangs from cables attached to the concrete post, so it appears as if it's floating in the air. It's thought to be safe, even in an 8.0 shake."

"Earthquakes your thing, young man?"

Perry looks at me, seeking permission to deliver what we refer to as an "expert ear bashing." I nod.

"I like earthquakes," he says. "My father called me Master Disaster. But I have other favorite things. I like creatures from the sea that are considered myths. The Loch Ness Monster, the Bunyip in Australia. We're going to Okanagan Lake to see the famous one there—the one called Ogopogo. *Ogopogo* means 'lake demon' in Canadian Aboriginal language.

"I'm very interested in Jackie Chan and his movies. He's incredible and does all his own stunts, which is unwise because the outtakes of every movie show him getting hurt over and over again. I think the old Chinese movie *Drunken Master II* is his best one, but I enjoy *Rush Hour* and *Shanghai Noon* as well. *The Karate Kid*—that was stupid. Jackie Chan doesn't perform karate. He's a kung-fu master. *Rumble in the Bronx* is excellent! And it was filmed in this city of Vancouver. No lie.

"The subject that I'm expert in is, of course, earthquakes. I have a seismometer and a seismograph, so I collect my own data. I've researched the biggest quakes in history. The one in Valdivia, Chile, in 1960, was an unbelievable 9.5 magnitude. To date, it is the biggest quake in history, although there could have been similar ones back in the time of the dinosaurs and during the first millennium. No one can say for sure. And I know about the San Francisco, California, earthquake in 1906 and, of course, Haiti this year. Over three hundred thousand people perished in Haiti. The one in Newcastle only killed thirteen people, but it is the only Australian quake in which people have died. And I know about the earthquake that occurred on Vancouver Island too—it was a 7.3."

Jim taps his hand on his thigh and whistles. "Wow. You're a supersmart guy, all right. I got a lotta questions I'd like to ask you. But I think there's something you oughta see first, eh."

Jim points to a building ahead. I've never seen a photo of it—didn't know of its existence until five minutes ago—but I know I'm gaining an eyeful of the Qube. It's a peculiar sight: a steel-and-glass hulk hovering six meters or so off the ground while the unseen cables above keep it fastened to its concrete core. Perry's in heaven. His mouth is agape. His hands are clasped together under his chin. He's a kid at a divine magic show. God has decided to try His hand at illusionism in downtown Vancouver.

"That's something, isn't it?" says Jim. "Hasn't been tested by a big shake yet."

Perry wriggles free of his awe to respond. "I read on Wikipedia that geologists are predicting a 37 percent chance of an 8.2-plus event and a 10 to 15 percent chance of a 9.0-plus event in the Pacific Northwest sometime in the next fifty years."

Jim shrugs. "Bah, bring it on. We don't mind a scrap. Like the economic meltdown—a real eleven on the scale, that one. They say it wasn't as bad here as down south, but hell, I'm still havin' to drive a cab on weekends." He catches my eye in the rearview mirror and smiles. "You gotta do what you gotta do, eh? Specially when someone in your family needs you to step up."

We take several right turns, doubling back from our Qube detour, then swing around a bend that skirts the Vancouver Convention Centre. An elegant mirrored tower and an assortment of expensive cars signal our arrival at the Pacifica West Hotel. A split second after he puts the emergency brake on, Jim is out of the car and unloading our gear. When a valet wearing a gray tunic and top hat approaches, Jim holds up an index finger. The valet stands post at a respectful distance, shifting from foot to foot. Jim lowers his hand and extends it toward me.

"Miss Justine, even though you're a Richter, I hope you enjoy your stay in our beautiful city."

"Thank you, Jim. We will," I reply. "And all the best to your son. He's pretty lucky to have a 'special' dad."

Jim inhales sharply, then doffs an imaginary cap. He turns to my brother. "Take care of your sister, young man."

Perry nods emphatically, then resumes his study of the large canopy shielding the Saabs and the Audis and the BMWs from the threat of Vancouver drizzle.

Jim Graydon smiles, waves and moves in behind the wheel. As he pulls away from the curb, I see a lit cigar lodged in the corner of his mouth.

·············●·············

A BROKEN PROMISE AWAITS AT CHECK-IN.

"There is a phone message for you, Ms. Richter."

"Oh. Okay."

"A gentleman called."

"What?"

"A gentleman called from Australia."

"You're kidding."

The figurine-like Asian clerk retrieves a piece of notepaper from beneath the desk and passes it over. It's from Marc.

Can we talk? Just a quick call.

Perry, returned from his observation of a three-stories-tall totem pole in the lobby, stares at me with brow clenched. "What are you reading?"

"A phone message."

"Who called you, Justine?"

"Marc."

"Mark Arm? The lead singer of Seattle grunge rock band Mudhoney, who were popular in the nineties?"

"Funny. No, Marc Paolini. Protagonist in Justine's version of *Sense and Sensibility*."

"What?"

"Never mind."

Perry moves closer and adopts a hypnotist's tone. "I don't understand your face at the moment, Justine. Are you angry? Sad? Confused?"

I scrunch the paper into a ball, stuff it into the hip pocket of my jeans. "It's my 'Let's go get room service' face."

On the way to the elevator, to prevent any further explorations of my face, I ask Perry about the totem pole. He launches into a recount of the stacked carvings, their colors and the animals each represents. He argues they're a lot easier to understand than a human expression.

I nod on cue to keep my brother talking and off the scent of my own thoughts. Marc phoning the hotel is something I hadn't expected. We had a deal—for the duration of this trip, we would be *incommunicado*. No emails, no phone calls, no Facebook. Not even a postcard.

He'd asked if I would miss him. I'd said I would miss his sleepy eyes and strong shoulders. The Friday night "freak show" movies and Sunday-morning omelets. I would miss his impromptu gifts, his spontaneous kazoo serenades. He would never be very far from my thoughts. It would be tough to lose connection for two weeks, but it would resume easily enough when I returned. The same couldn't be said for my relationship with Perry. How it had been since Dad died—some might argue how it had been for nineteen years—would never be the same after the trip. This was precious time, deserving of my full and undivided attention. This was Pez and Just Jeans time. The last time it would ever be *just us*.

You can handle a fortnight without me, I'd said. *You know the saying: absence makes the heart blah-blah-blah.*

Marc had nodded, assured me he would comply. *It's okay*, he'd said with a forced, faintly sulky smile. *I know I'm not the only man in your life.* He'd withheld his usual array of affections, preferring a dutiful hug and a kiss on the forehead. He'd done the same at the departure gate.

And now he wants to talk. *Now*. At the very time I need him to be strong and secure enough to stay out of the pool, he sprints in from the change rooms and dive-bombs the shallow end. What is so important that it can't wait? I have a hunch.

The Appointment.

We don't see eye to eye on that one. He thinks I should avoid it and come home after the Seattle leg of our trip.

What's the point? were his exact words during our most recent argument. *Do you really think it'll make a difference? Actually, skip that. Do you really think it's deserved?*

Marc reminds me of Dad in that way—people are people, and that's the way it is. If someone wronged you, hurt you, let you down in ways unimagined, don't dwell on it. Don't try to explain it. You might fool yourself into thinking they can be different, or that time or money or distance or therapy can magically transform their DNA. Just move on as they stand still.

Dad liked to compare people to presents: *You can change the paper and the ribbon and the card, but you can't change what's inside. And what's inside—maybe you want to keep it, maybe you want to throw it away.*

Marc doesn't want us unwrapping what awaits in Vancouver. Sorry, hon. Some people in this world are prepared to give a bad gift a second chance.

Approaching our room on the sixteenth floor, I hope extravagance will ease my mind. One step inside the door brings it home—the suite is a designer version of Ali Baba's cave. Perry and I stand rigid in the center of the room for ten seconds or more, silently drinking it in. The windows extend from floor to ceiling and serve up 180 degrees of water-and-mountain panorama. The TV is not much smaller than our Brisbane fridge. The only item missing from the bar is a cocktail waiter. I think to myself:

This is wrong. We are misplaced. We are the jigsaw piece separated from the puzzle for which it was designed, trying to fit where it doesn't belong.

"What do you think, Pez?" I murmur. "Bit better than the old holiday house at Rainbow Beach?"

Perry offers three big nods. "Is this what Fair Go will be like?"

"If it is, then I'm coming with you."

"Really?"

"No. I'd cramp your style."

Perry ponders my meaning, then shrugs and walks out onto the balcony. He returns thirty seconds later, clenching and unclenching his hands. "You can see Stanley Park from the deck. Some of the scenes in the *Twilight: New Moon* movie were shot there. No lie. I didn't notice any vampires. But I did see a cruise ship at the dock—Holland America. I also saw a man walking along the pier, talking on his phone. He climbed into a red-and-white aircraft and took off, no passengers on board. Maybe he was learning to fly. Or maybe he stole the plane."

"That's great. You want to check out your room, see if it's got a butler or something?"

Mention of the phone guy reminds me of Marc's message. A little temperance has entered my thoughts. We are novices here—all of us—Marc especially.

A girlfriend minus a family, save for a special-needs twin brother—it would be a shock to the system for anyone. Until my appearance on the scene, Marc Andre Paolini had enjoyed something of a sheltered ride. The baby in a tight-knit family of five; parents living, present and lovingly married for twenty-nine years; two older brothers who looked out for their "Marky Mark" during school and university. By any definition, Life had been kind to him, patting him on the head and whispering sweet nothings in his ear.

In this idyllic existence, would he somehow have accumulated the real and lasting experience of being alone, of having loved ones unreachable? Not that I've seen. We are polar opposites on that count. Father passed, mother gone, brother like sand falling through fingers. My nineteen years can be measured by the spaces and the silences of my relationships. It's been standard for me, and it's black to Marc's white. We are a new version of *Sense and Sensibility*.

Close and Closeted.

"Okay," I mutter, inspecting the landline phone for messages and finding none. "One call we can overlook."

After a token effort to unpack, we doze, me in the bedroom and Perry on the couch.

········•········

18 January 1993

I think we'll go somewhere fun tomorrow—just you, me and Perry. Maybe Redcliffe. Go and have a paddle on the beach there. Grab a Bubble O' Bill afterward. Well, not for Perry, of course. He's a Chicos man. Yeah, a trip out of the house for the three of us is the ticket. Give us all a chance to take a deep breath.

Justine, I don't know how much of last night you will remember when you're older. If it does grab hold in your memory, know that it wasn't your or your brother's fault. Mum's not coping real well with Perry's tantrums. She sort of relies on you to be the good girl all the time, which is unfair. You're not even out of diapers, for crying out loud! Last night I didn't get home until the fireworks were pretty much over. (Jeez, I wish I hadn't got stuck on Hale Street. I might've been able to stop it from getting out of hand.) But from what I gather, Mum got hit. It was an accident—Perry threw his head back while she was restraining him and he hit her in the mouth. That did it. She was bleeding, she was upset. She felt like nothing made sense and that everything was falling apart. She took it out on the toys and the walls.

Anyway, it's a new day. The screaming has stopped. The tears gone. The busted stuff will be fixed. And maybe Mum, with a bit of space, a bit less hurt and a bit of twenty-twenty hindsight, might have a clearer view of the world.

Maybe she'll begin to admit the truth about Perry. Blind Freddy could see that what he's got isn't going away. It's not some phase. It's not a speed bump he's run into. It's the way he is. The way he'll continue to be.

It's not him, but it's in him.

··········●··········

I'M WOKEN BY STREAMING SUNLIGHT and the grunts, whips and various other sound effects of kung-fu fighting. The portable DVD player sitting on the desk has *Rumble in the Bronx* showing, volume turned to the max. The movie has arrived at its infamous scene, where Jackie Chan jumps from a bridge and onto a passing hovercraft—the result in real life being a broken ankle.

"Perry?"

My brother is not in his usual position—leaning forward, face less than a handspan from the tiny screen.

"Pez! Where are you, mate?"

Several more shouts and a search of both room and balcony deliver nothing. My heart feels a small squeeze of panic. Skewed thoughts spawn and multiply. He's taken off, on his own, in a strange city. He has no money, no phone. He's lost. He's freaking out on some street corner. Ohmygod, Perry! Jesus! Did you really need basic instructions tattooed to your forehead? Don't leave the hotel without me, don't leave the room without me, don't do *anything* without me.

I snap the band at my wrist. The kneejerk, bad-voice-in-my-head stuff isn't helping. Like Dad used to say: *Think it through before you throw yourself or somebody else off the Story Bridge.* Sitting down at the desk, I try to tune out the anger and fear. I need to think logically. Perry wouldn't have left on a whim. He's not an absconder— never has been. He's also conscious of others, the fact they have thoughts and feelings and physical responses influenced by his actions. You wouldn't ever say he's fully empathetic—he'd be here in this room if he were—but he's certainly not oblivious to needs beyond his own. And, in the end, he is a grown man and he does think for himself. It's why he had final say in the Fair Go decision. It's why he'll have the right to veto anything proposed at The Appointment.

My rational self is validated during the third inspection of Perry's room. A sheet of paper with Pacifica West letterhead pokes out of the top pocket of his carry-on.

I am going to the pool, Justine. I didn't want to wake you up, so I left this note. It is provided so that you know

where I am and you won't worry. Remember, too, I am an
excellent swimmer.

Perry Richter

When I arrive at the pool, Perry has the entire facility to himself. He's making the most of it—running in from the side and leaping feetfirst into the water.

"You missed the hovercraft," I say when he surfaces.

He stares blankly at me for an instant, then smiles. "Ha, you are joking!" He lifts his foot out of the water and points to his ankle. "Didn't break!" He vaults out of the pool and stands in front of me, hands on hips. It's eerie how much he resembles Dad, with his slicked hair and broad chest and loud boardshorts. And his feet— wide as they are long. Feet like that keep a person fastened to the earth.

"You found my note," he says.

"Eventually."

"What do you mean?"

"It took a long time to find it, brother. It wasn't in the most obvious place."

"But I wanted to make it easy, so I put it where my togs and towel were packed. I enjoy swimming…I thought you would remember."

"I didn't forget you enjoyed swimming, Pez. I just didn't know you'd *gone* swimming. When I woke up and

57

you weren't around, I needed that info fast. It would've been better to put the note on my bedside table or maybe the desk. Not in the place where your gear was packed!"

He doesn't get the reasoning; it's like a trapeze just out of reach, brushing his fingertips with every swing through. He walks forward, avoiding eye contact. He wraps his arms around me and squashes me against his wet body.

"Are you making a mountain out of a mold hill, Just Jeans?"

"No. Are you seeing me, Pez?"

"Yes, but I honestly think this is a mold hill."

"It's not."

"A tiny little hill covered in mold."

"For God's sake, Perry, it's mole! *Mole!*"

"Mole?" He pulls back and peeks out of the corner of his narrowed eyes. He makes a show of examining the skin on his arms and shoulders. Torso and legs. Inner thighs.

"Before you drop your pants, Dr. Joke, I'll tell you exactly how it went down," I say, dabbing at my jeans and T-shirt with a towel. "When I woke up and you weren't there, I was very worried. Then, when I found your note and saw you here at the pool, I was very relieved. And now I'm back to normal."

"You mean happy?"

I wipe the water from his forehead. "Sure, why not."

He nods, gives me a hug, then throws himself into the deep end, shouting some form of kung-fu battle cry.

·············●●●···········

WE STAY AT THE POOL until late afternoon. I split time between watching Perry's indefatigable stuntman act and reading *Robinson Crusoe*. Lazing in a lounge chair, absorbing the pleasant but stunted rays of a tepid Canadian sun, the castaway's plight makes me feel small and blessed. The mold hills of Justine Richter's world don't seem so scary next to island isolation. The new beginnings of the next month don't measure up to a proper tale of base survival. I run a hand over the paperback's front-cover image of footprints in the sand. Yes, I can read Defoe and count myself lucky. But could my brother say the same?

I watch him perform a mock news report on the miraculous discovery of Ogopogo in the Pacifica West pool, and then my thoughts drift. Fleeting pictures of a marooned Perry in the Fair Go Community Village take hold. His clothes are torn and dirty. His face is sunburned bright red. He has a beard down to his belt line.

He's killing goats and building a shelter and figuring out which plants he can eat. He's a ragged Extrasensory Perry, Master Disaster with an edge. I laugh—a hollow rasp that comes from a place of disquiet rather than mirth—and set the book down on the concrete. I tell my brother he has five more minutes.

Back at the suite, I surf the net on Perry's iPad while he watches *The Tuxedo*. There are a few diverting articles from the major daily, *Vancouver Sun*, and several more from something called *The Tyee*. A story about a former hockey player's charity golf tournament reminds me of the conversation with Jim Graydon. I google Byron Dafoe. The article references are many and varied—most stem from his playing days, some highlight his fundraising work—but it's the photographs of him decked out in his goalie gear I find particularly fascinating. The size and volume of the equipment is unlike anything I've ever seen. The leg pads are like mattresses. The upper-body protection puts the Michelin Man's bulk to shame. I think back to Graydon's mention of his son—he wears all *that* and he doesn't even play? It strikes me that there may be some symmetry in this scenario—a disabled child donning the ultimate armor as his everyday wear. He might even be able to dole out some comeuppance to the bullies with the big stick he carries.

We have room service for dinner. Around eight, I watch the second half of *The Tuxedo* with Perry. It's not Jackie Chan's finest hour, but it's the movie I've seen least often. Against my better judgment, I can recite verbatim large chunks of *Rush Hour* and *Rush Hour 2*. And it's possible I've acquired conversational Cantonese from endless *Drunken Master II* reruns. When the credits roll, Perry announces he's going to bed. He gives me a long hug that borders on a boxer's clinch.

"I won't cause you to worry again while we are in North America," he says, resting his chin on my shoulder. "And you won't have any concerns when I move away and become independent."

I kiss his cheek. "Get some good sleep. Big day tomorrow."

He disappears into his room. As per usual, he keeps a light on in case he wakes during the night.

················●···········

I OPEN MY FATHER'S JOURNAL and turn to its most thumbed page. The entry it displays must be read before making the call. I know the words, but I need to see them. Stare them down.

..........●..........

30 November 1994

Your mother won't be living with us anymore. We had a huge row last night. (How you and your brother slept through it, I'll never know.) It was the final straw for both of us. She wanted to go away for a month to some yoga camp in the middle of Woop Woop. I told her this was not the time—so soon after getting the word on Perry—to be traipsing off to some hippie hotel in the bush to stare at your navel and play silly buggers under a full moon. We need to stick together, be there for each other. Move forward and live our lives. She went nuts. Yelled at me for a good half hour. She reckons I'm a hypocrite, that I am never there for her, that I am a selfish and cold prick. That I don't understand the first thing about living her life, and it's never going to change. Things are never going to "move forward." She was always going to be an overwhelmed mother, I was always going to be a crappy husband, and Perry was always going to be handicapped and dependent on others. She said she couldn't live a life that offered no chance to find herself, no chance to chase her own dreams. She said she'd rather die. Then she packed a couple of bags and left.

On the way out, I told her: "Good luck finding yourself doing nude jumping jacks with the tree huggers. Don't bother keeping in touch. We'll be fine."

I didn't sleep the rest of the night. When you got up, I told you Mum had gone away and she wouldn't be living here anymore. You thought about it for a minute, and then you gave me a hug. "You're staying, aren't you, Daddy?" you asked. I said I wasn't going anywhere, I'd always be here with the two of you. Then you said you had to go and tell Perry, and you ran off to his room. And I tried to swallow the lump in my throat while getting breakfast together and listening to you explain to your brother that it was just going to be the three of us from now on.

............●●●●●●●●●●●●●

I LAY A HAND ON the phone. A film of perspiration gathers between my palm and the plastic receiver. My heart gallops around my chest. The four-year-old girl in me wants to slide out of the chair, sink to the floor and stay there, Perry style, placing the onus on others to re-engage me with the world. I can't indulge her. She doesn't know what the nineteen-year-old knows.

I stare at the ten digits scribbled down on a piece of scrap paper. It's a local number, sent along with our mother's most recent letter, which arrived three weeks ago. It was the first time she'd provided any source of contact beyond a return postal address. Till that day, there'd really been no need—we'd assumed the role of pen pals for three years and I'd only shared with her the dot points of my life: the piñata calamity of my sixteenth birthday; the breakdown over Dad's diagnosis; the standing ovation I received for a speech at school; the decision for Perry to move into a supported residence. She'd shared with me her exploits as a yoga studio owner and teacher; the personal best she'd achieved for some local climb called the Grouse Grind; the succession of failed relationships with "douche bags"; her tentative proposal to return to Australia and earn a place back in our lives.

She'd shared her number.

I look over at Perry's room. Light streams from the crack under the door, undisturbed by any shadowy presence. There's no movement, no sound beyond muted, rhythmic snoring. Good. I don't want him to know about this, not until the Okanagan and Seattle are done. I turn back to the phone and lift the receiver from its cradle. My fingers prickle as I punch out the sequence. The ringing on the other end of the line commences and I feel my body dividing like a cell into two entities: caller and observer. I pray some semblance of recognizable English will form on my tongue.

"Hello. You've reached the home of Leonie Orr. Sorry I can't take your call right now…"

No chance to find herself.

"…If you'd like to leave your name and phone number, I'll get back to you as soon as I can…"

No chance to chase her own dreams.

"Thank you and have a wonderful day."

She'd rather die.

The beep sounds.

"Um, yeah. This is Justine, your…It's Justine. Just ringing to let you know we've arrived and we're staying at the downtown hotel. We'll be on the road tomorrow. I've got a Canadian number—it is 778-232-4953. I also gave you the landline number for the place we're staying at in Peachland. So, give me a ring and we can confirm our…get-together. Okay, yeah. Hope to hear from you soon…Leonie. Bye."

I kill the call and flop back into the chair. Things would probably be a hell of a lot easier if she'd never put pen to paper, if she'd remained a ghost in our lives. But, after all these years, why should anything be easy now? And isn't it better to be haunted by ghosts of the living rather than the dead?

In the cavernous spaces, Dad's words buzz like mosquitoes: *Don't bother keeping in touch. We'll be fine.*

·········●··········

DREAMING AGAIN.

It's not like last time. The primal energy that rocked the island is gone. The blue-green water is calm. I'm still Crusoe, but with one significant rejig—an ice-hockey goaltender's full regalia has replaced the castaway rags. I'm still stuck to the boat's seat, but I'm not desperate to get away.

Perry/Xury has emerged from the wash and is standing onshore. He waves and begins walking south along the beach. My boat moves with him. The source of power is unknown until I look ahead. Dad is in the seat opposite, rowing. He's bare-chested and wearing orange-and-lime-green boardies. His muscles bunch and flex with each stroke. He's in the best shape of his life, a good twenty kilograms heavier than the husk of a man that died in my arms.

"The boy chose to go, didn't he," he says.

I nod. "He said he had to. He said we couldn't survive like this."

"That's true." Dad grunts and quickens his pace. The boat heaves forward. "He's not alone over there."

I turn back to land. A lone figure at the far end of the shoreline is walking toward an oblivious Perry/Xury. From this distance, it's difficult to tell if the visitor is male or female, friend or foe, real or imagined. I pull my helmet off and squint at the shape. The trudging body remains anonymous.

Then the scene dissolves in the Seltzer-like rays of a new dawn.

...........•••••...........

30 January 1996

First day of school! You guys looked fantastic in your uniforms and carrying your schoolbags. You did such a good job, Justine, holding Perry's hand, telling him what was going on, keeping him calm. It needn't be all the time, though. Like we talked about last night, you don't have to be Grandma Poss and use bush magic to turn Perry invisible to protect him and keep him safe. You still need to make your own friends and do your own thing.

We made it to Year One, hey? Since your mother left, there have been a few times when I thought I might end up going off the deep end myself. Your brother is a handful, that's for sure. The difficulties with his potty training. The sleeping issues. The meltdowns at the shops. Trying to get him to eat a bloody vegetable. But just when I'd feel like I'd reached the end of my tether, something would happen to make it all fade into the background. And, almost always, my little tree frog, you'd be smack bang in the center of it.

Like last week, when he hurt himself on the mini-trampoline. I tried to soothe him every way I knew how so I could inspect the damage. I even sang that "Thomas the Tank Engine" song that makes me want to attach live jumper cables to my ears. Nothing worked. Then you came into the room. You went straight to the toy box, pulled out this little alien monster I'd never even seen before, brought it over to him and, without a word said, held it close to his face so he could see. The first glimpse he got of it—or maybe it was the first glimpse he got of you?—he settled down immediately. It was a magic trick Grandma Poss would've been proud of.

············●············

16 November 1996

Perry's really beginning to "get" some things now. He's giving out hugs on his own, without any prompting. He's able to put together the picture exchange cards in a sequence and then say the words if he wants a drink or a biscuit. Occasionally, he'll sing an entire "Bananas in Pyjamas" song from start to finish. He's learning numbers, counting in twos and fives and tens. Running around and copying you and the neighbors' kids when you're all playing Sticky Glue in the afternoons—that's the time of his life right now. He's going good. He's a lot sharper than people give him credit for.

He sees stuff, too. Feels stuff. You agree, Jus? I know extra-keen senses can be part and parcel of his condition, but there are times when it's something more. Not a "gift" or anything like that—we're not living in The Twilight Zone *here. Just more of a connection to the world around him. A deeper connection. Like a couple of weeks ago when I found him lying on his back in the yard. I asked him what he was up to and he started singing the "Shaky Shaky" Wiggles song and patting the grass. And he kept repeating it no matter what I said, as if he were trying to make a point. I didn't figure it out until the next day when I saw in the local rag they'd been using explosives at the quarry and the reverberations could be felt over a sixteen-kilometer radius. I was gobsmacked. Could he be in tune with something like that? Is it possible? The more I think about it, the more I reckon it's par for the course. Things most of the rest of the world wouldn't be aware of—he's aware of them. He notices them.*

Or maybe it's just what kids do and adults forget.

··········•••••··········

10 January 1999

This holiday has had its share of firsts. It's the first time you and your brother have seen Rainbow Beach— the place where, as a young bloke, I learned to surf and got up to some things that aren't fit to be retold in my daughter's journal. First time you two have stayed in a hotel. First time—since you were babies, anyway—that you've shared a bed. (And I don't think you want to do it again for a while, hey, Justine? Perry could lift the paint off a low-flying bomber with his snoring.) And I know it's not the first time, but it seems like the first time I've really noticed…I feel happy.

If I'm not mistaken, you guys are happy too. Your brother's been good and settled here, hasn't he? I was worried what might happen with him being out of routine and everything being so different. But it's been a fairly smooth ride. He's learned some new phrases. (I'm not sure "topless girl" is one I'll encourage him to use in public.) He loves hopping on the surf mat and riding a wave. And how good was it when he grabbed a piece of the crumbed cod we got from Harry's off my plate and ate it? Totally out of the blue!

I've gotta say, your question at tea did a number on me. "Dad, how come you don't have another wife yet?"

Jeez, eight years old and already giving me a hard time about my love life! My answer last night probably didn't explain things too well, so I'll try again here. I'm not against getting properly involved with someone again. Things turned out badly with your mother, but I'm not automatically thinking it would turn out badly with the next woman. It's possible I could get together with someone in the future. When might that be? I don't have a clue. Probably not any time soon, seeing as I'm not really keeping a constant eye out. I've got more than enough on my plate, courtesy of you two. The Dan Richter Dating Service is a distant last on the priority list. And if somebody did come along... Well, she'd have to be pretty special to fit in with us. I'm not going to let any old scrubber from the street into our little family. You guys deserve the best. And if the best isn't on offer, then I'd rather go without.

........•........

20 March 2001

One night down, two to go. This is the longest you've ever been away from us, Justine. School camps in the past were overnight or a couple of nights. Three is hard. We miss you. Perry keeps saying, "Is Just Jeans coming?

Is Just Jeans coming?" Maybe he'll finally have the proper pronunciation of your name worked out by the time you're back. For my part, this is a good reminder never to take you for granted. The stuff you do around here…it's just incredible, really. Laundry, cleaning, helping Perry with his homework. And more besides. I don't know what I'd do without you. But I don't say that to make you feel guilty for having a little R&R. I'm all for it. It'll be good for you to be around your friends and doing fun stuff for an extended time. God knows, you deserve it.

In a way, this is good practice for the future. The two boys, playing house, sharing the bachelor pad. At some point in this new century, you're going to move out and have your own life. And, as much as I'd like to say the same for your brother, as much as he's improved over the years, I can't see it happening. He's going to need some level of support throughout his life. It's my job to provide it. He's my responsibility. You might argue with me about that, but it's true. You are Perry's sister, not his parent. You love him and I know you always will. But you never need think you are his keeper. As the two of you grow into adulthood, you can walk beside him rather than carry him.

Ah, my little tree frog, all of a sudden it's the 2000s. I'm not so sure you're little anymore.

Think I'll finish here for this entry—I've got a whole lot of extra laundry to do, haven't I?

..........●●●●..........

12 December 2003

Your marks are tremendous, Justine! I don't think the phone book has as many A's as you do. You've always been a very good student, but this year you've taken off. It seems like the further you go in school, the smarter you become. Maybe it's because you've had to grow up quicker than your school-mates. You've missed out on much of the early teenage rubbish due to real-world experience. Or maybe it's my A-grade Richter genes coming through. My money's on that.

The sky's the limit for you, Justine. You can do anything. There are a lot of scared people in this world, due to those lunatics who fly planes into buildings and blow up innocent people and invade foreign countries and make up stories about weapons and refuse to try a little kindness for anyone who's different from themselves. But you shouldn't be scared. You've got nothing to fear, from anything or anyone. You may not have seen the worst of the world—not by a long shot—but you know struggle. You know that life can be a kick in the guts more often than a pat on the back. And did it get the better of you? Did you end up angry and bitter and hurt? Did you pack your bags, then up and leave, never to come back? No way! You've come out of it with an A-plus. An A-plus mind and, more important, an A-plus heart.

Perry's so lucky to have you as his sister. There are a lot of kids out there who wouldn't have a twin sister and a role model and a friend all rolled into one curly-haired package. I feel bad for them. I really do. If only there were more of you to go around.

·············●●·············

23 April 2005

So, you think we were a bit hard on that scrawny lad you brought home? What's his name? Paul? That's right— Paul. To be honest, I thought he got off lightly. I only hinted once that he should change his last name. (Sexton is not a surname my daughter should have any association with.) And Perry only asked him a thousand questions about earthquakes. Master Disaster let him off lightly, all right. Joking aside, Jus, he seems like a good kid. I hope he doesn't break your nearly-fifteen-year-old heart too bad.

I'm sorry I never sat you down and talked about love and relationships. Not really the done thing with dads (maybe not even single dads). If we had given it a go at some point, what decent advice could I have given you?

Maybe this, I suppose: Know what you don't want.

Your mother gave me a good lesson in that. After she bailed on us, I had a very solid idea of things I wanted to avoid. There were more than a few things, too. You might say a few too many. Ah, well, I don't regret being too fussy if it meant you guys stayed clear of Your Mother—Round Two. God knows, I haven't been perfect as a dad, but I stayed the course and I always tried to put you and your brother first. And that's going to continue, not because I'm a martyr or a saint or a much hairier Mother Teresa. No, it's because I know what I don't want. I don't want the two of you to miss out on the best years of your life. Or to be in a home where you're an afterthought. Or to blame yourselves for bad things that happen. Or to think love can't be trusted.

Love is reliable. You can depend on it.

PERRY

JUSTINE AND I ARE IN A Chevrolet Cobalt, speeding along the Trans-Canada Highway. So much of what I see is strange. Cars driving on the right-hand side of the road, of course. There are no trailers, just large motorhomes called Winnebago and CanaDream. The speed limit signs are square and don't have a red circle. The words *SPEED LIMIT* are actually written on them. What is the reason for that? Do North Americans need exact instructions like I do when I'm working at Troy's car wash and a customer wants detailing? And I am on the driver's side! There should be a steering wheel in my hands! That wouldn't be wise. During my first lesson with Justine last year, in the empty car park at the rear of Brookfair Shopping Center, I ran into three trolleys and a traffic island. No lie. Justine said one lesson per year was more than enough.

With all this new information surrounding me, I would be quite anxious if this were a normal day. This isn't a normal day—this is the start of our big adventure. Ogopogo's home is our first destination. Thinking about what might happen over the next two days makes the strangeness of the highway shrink until it's only mildly annoying, like a mosquito buzzing around my head.

I look over at Justine. She is herself—pretty and clever. Her hair is pulled up into a bun and she's wearing the shirt that has a drawing of William Shakespeare (Justine calls him Bill or Baldy Bill) riding a surfboard and holding a skull. It's hard to tell what her face is showing about her feelings because she has sunglasses on. I can only see one side of her head because she is watching the road. I guess she is calm and settled, but I could be wrong. I don't know what she's feeling inside; her heart could be racing, her stomach might be flip-flopping. You can never be completely sure.

I like observing Justine when she's doing something important and having to concentrate. I can watch and learn and not worry that she'll speak suddenly or do something surprising. And she won't say things like "Focus on me" or "Are you seeing me?" Sometimes I pull faces at her. When she catches me, without looking she says, "You need a makeover again, Pez?" Then I do the stupid duck lips I've seen lots of girls doing on the *FAIL* blog.

After three minutes I look away. (It's creepy if you watch someone for too long, especially a woman.) I pull out the folded road map of British Columbia.

"We goin' the right way?" asks Justine.

I see a green road sign, then give three nods. "Hope is seventy-six kilometers away."

"First stop: Hope. I like the sound of that."

No lie, I think it's a dumb name for a town. But Australian towns have ridiculous names, too:

Blackbutt

Poowong

Mount Buggery

I start giggling and I can't stop. When Dad was alive, he said my laughing fits were like having a cockatoo in the house. *Raaark! Raaark!* He said I should wear a yellow rubber glove on my head so I could look the part. *Raaark! Raaark!* Justine and I would flap our pretend wings and Dad would say silly sentences in a parrot's voice. And we would all laugh together.

Here, today, in our Chevrolet Cobalt on Trans-Canada Highway 1, Justine doesn't ask me what the joke is, she just joins in. Sometimes I think she's "extrasensory" like me, or she's got lots of funny stories in her head. I *love* hearing her laugh. The same as I *hate* hearing her cry.

When we leave Highway 1 and turn onto Highway 5, I'm tired and I want to take a nap. My body has no energy. My brain is packed tight, like the bales of hay at the plant nursery near our house. Justine is not surprised. She talks about jet lag, how it "impairs your functioning" and "makes it hard to concentrate" and "messes with your body clock." It can even upset your toileting. She says not to worry—it goes away after a day or two, or a week, or, in bad cases, a month. I tell her I'm glad because I don't need another disability. The one I've got comes with a lifetime guarantee, like my hair color and my fingerprints and my excellent ability to make jokes.

When I wake up, we are pulling into the parking lot of a fast-food restaurant called Dairy Queen. In front of us, just past the turnoff road, is a wide river. Behind are large mountains covered in green forest. In my imagination, the houses and the shops and the streets are being bullied; the mountains are standing over them like a cruel gang, attempting to force them into the water. From my research, I know the mountains have been cruel in real life. In 1965, the Hope Slide happened at Johnson Peak, a few kilometers southeast of the town. It buried two cars and a tanker truck under mud and rock that was eighty-five meters deep and three kilometers wide. Rescuers could only find two of the four victims killed. For a while, people thought it had been caused by an earthquake because it registered seismically, but it was just a slip, like the one that trapped Stuart Diver in the Thredbo landslide. As I climb out of the car, I'm not sure if it's the thought of buried bodies or the cool breeze that makes me shiver. A sudden gust blows the hood of my sweater over my head.

"Welcome to Hope, brother." Just Jeans smiles and locks the Cobalt, ensuring no one will steal it while we are inside.

·············●●●············

THE MENU ABOVE THE COUNTER IS SCARY.

Burgers, chips, salads, a chicken wrap—these are fine. The hot dog is okay, too. I tried a sausage on bread last October at Bunnings. But then I look closer and find lots of confusing details. There is mayo on the burgers. The beef is from the Canadian province of Alberta. One of the sandwiches is "Iron Grilled!" I begin rubbing my hands down the front of my jeans, digging my thumbs in with each stroke. There were a lot of unfamiliar sights on the highway, and thinking about Ogopogo made me feel better—but this is different. This is *food*. It goes into my mouth, into my digestive system and then into my entire body. I need to properly know what I'm eating. What if the mayo gives me an allergy? What if Alberta has mad cows? What if the iron grill allows metal fragments into my bloodstream?

"Perry, you okay?"

I suck the air through my teeth and hunch my shoulders.

"How about you go and sit over at that table near the front window," whispers Justine. "I'll get you something that's okay. Trust me."

The edges of my vision have rounded and gone gray. It's like I'm looking through a telescope that has a dirty lens. There are people all around—no doubt they are watching me—the small girl standing beside me in the pink jacket and holding a Barbie in her right hand; the overweight couple wearing shiny belt buckles and cowboy hats; the group of teenagers comparing their tans.

They think I have a problem. They don't realize they are the ones with the problem—they've eaten the food! And it's too late for them now. One by one, they drop to the floor: first the cowboy, then his wife, then the teenagers. The girl watches the others fall before the pain hits her like a kung-fu kick. She screams, pulls the head off her Barbie and stumbles, smacking her forehead on the edge of the vending machine before going down. The floor is full of dying people now. Twisting, groaning. Foaming at the mouth. They grab at their throats, knowing that's where the pain is worst, but not knowing why. I know why. The iron grill fragments in the food have gathered there. They've come together and bonded, forming sharp metal pieces. Blades. Bulges begin to form in the victims' necks. They grow larger and larger. And the bigger they get, the more pointed they become. The cowboy woman is the first to have the blade break through the skin—the *pop* reminds me of overheated porridge in the microwave. Others follow. Soon, the tiles are gobbled up by a tsunami of blood. I don't want to see any more. I don't want to think about the Dairy Queen disaster. I want to lie down and let all the heavy weights in my head fall through the floor. I want to—

"Pez," Justine whispers right in my ear. "Keep it together, bud."

I hold my breath for a few seconds, then focus on my shoes. The blood has vanished. The surrounding floor has streaks and scuff marks and a small yellow sign saying *Caution—Wet Floor.*

"Trust me. I got it. Just Jeans to the rescue, hey?"

I turn slightly and command my feet to move. For a long time there is no response. Then they follow my order, stepping once, twice. By the time I sit down at the table, my anxiety has returned to a steady hum. I can process better now.

Just Jeans saves the day again.

I lay my head on the table. Its surface is cool on my cheek.

Just Jeans saves the day AGAIN.

It sucks being a hassle. I want to be brave and strong, like Jackie Chan in *Drunken Master II* when he is attacked by the gang of men with axes. Coping when things get intense is very hard. No lie. All the difficulties crowd my brain and yell and scream and smash into each other. The good things I try to fill my mind with—Ogopogo, for example—they get pushed out the same way convection in the Earth's mantle gets expelled and causes earthquakes or volcanic eruptions. So then I am caught. I am caught in a tremor, and my sister is the only person who can stop the shaking.

It's not fair to her. Things will be better when I move to Fair Go. Justine won't have to save the day anymore. She will live a normal life. She will be free. And I will find solutions to my own problems because I won't have my sister to rely on. Relying on yourself—that's what everyday people do; that is what it means to be independent.

Perry Richter saves the day.

That is the future.

Justine arrives at the table, holding a tray. She hands me a basket with my meal arranged neatly inside. "There you go. Chicken strips and chips. No weirdness."

I poke the food with my finger. It is recognizable. I pick up one of the strips, hold it to my mouth, nibble. It's good. As I swallow, I turn my head and spy Justine at the edges of my vision. She has her hands fully wrapped around her burger. She also has two napkins placed over the top of the meal in her basket, like she's performing a magic trick. And it sort of *is* a magic trick—I can't see any of the food she's eating. It's as if the food has disappeared.

"Thank you," I say, and Justine winks because her mouth is too full to speak.

For a while, we eat and don't converse. Most of the time, I look outside. The wind is stronger. Leaves of different colors—red, yellow, orange, brown, pink—fly through the air and along the sidewalk. Seven people walk past, all of them wearing shorts, T-shirts and thongs. The river is lumpy. Justine notices me staring at the water.

"Looks full of Ogopogos today," she says. "All coming to see the town of Hope."

I wipe my mouth with a napkin, fold it, place it in the basket. "You're not right in the noggin."

Justine snorts. She lifts her index finger up and twirls it around her ear to indicate she's crazy. She crosses her arms over her chest, puts on a stupid voice and says, "Ooh, so many Ogopogos. Get me out of this straitjacket so I can have a swim with them!"

I laugh, and then we go back to being quiet for a while. When we've both finished our meals and only scraps of food are left, Jus asks me an interesting question.

"What is it about sea monsters, Pez? Why are you into them so much?"

It's not something I've ever been asked before—not by Justine or Dad or the teachers I had at school.

Thinking about the answer takes a few minutes. Justine doesn't stare, doesn't repeat the question. She knows I need a moment to think and organize a response. By the time I am ready to reply, she's cleaned up our table and the rubbish is in the bin.

"There are two reasons," I say. "The first is because they are excellent at hiding. They've survived for thousands of years and no one has caught them. And the second reason is they've learned to survive even though the world is confusing and difficult for them."

Justine's face changes. Her eyes widen. Her forehead creases. Her lips pull to one side. "That's...That makes a lot of sense." Her face changes again. It squashes a little and her mouth stretches. I know this look—Dad used to call it "cheeky chops." "Hiding, hey? So how come you don't like Sasquatch and Bigfoot?"

It's my turn to snort. "They're not real. They're just people dressed up in hairy suits."

Justine dabs her index finger on her tongue and draws a line in the air. "Well played, Mr. Richter."

I don't exactly know what that means, or why her voice sounded like a villain on TV. But there's no time to figure it out—we're ready to leave the Dairy Queen. And when she puts an arm around my shoulders, I know it's not something I should be worried about.

●●●●●●●●●●●●●●●●●●●●●●

"MARC…MARC! WE HAD A DEAL, REMEMBER? YES, yes, I know you think it was important to call, but this trip is more important, okay? *Much* more important."

I returned from the toilet to find Justine leaning against the steering wheel, head pressed against her forearm. She is talking on her phone. To begin with, I didn't know who she was talking to. I know now. Her face is hidden, but her slumped body and the tone of her voice tell me she is not enjoying the conversation. The fun we were sharing on our drive has disappeared.

I knew something uncomfortable was coming—I should have been prepared. When we first stopped, I didn't like the dark-colored, all-metal toilet building. It looked like a prison, or one of those observation huts where scientists watch nuclear explosions from a long distance away. I did a quick seismic reading on the ground beside the car.

"Earth behaving?" asked Justine. She spoke over her shoulder as she walked between two parked Dodge Ram trucks toward the toilet.

"I'm not sure," I replied.

She waved and opened the door to the block, which had a jammed lock and graffiti written on it. I did a second reading, this time placing the seismometer on the gravel at the edge of the paved parking lot. The result was no different from the first, but I felt *incorrect*, like I'd watched *The Accidental Spy* without any subtitles.

And I still feel that way now, only worse. Justine leans back in her seat, changes the phone to her other ear. "Marc, I do know how you feel about it. I knew the week before we got on the plane! You made your feelings very clear and your concerns have been duly noted. It doesn't change our plans…"

I can see most of her face now—it's red and glistening. The muscles in her cheek and jaw are tense.

"You're worried—I get it. You're looking out for me and Pez, you don't want me—us—to get hurt. That's very nice, Marc, very noble. You're being the good, dutiful boyfriend. You're also being the interfering, frustrating boyfriend…"

I don't think she is going to cry. That is a relief. I don't cope well when she cries.

"Do that. Take some time to think it over…Yes, try to see it from my perspective. Please…That's sweet…Okay, bye."

She presses the button to end the call and says four swearwords quickly, one after the other. She begins massaging her temples.

"All we need right now is a bit of time and space—not a guardian angel hanging over our shoulders. Right?"

"Right," I say. I don't really understand what Justine is asking, but I suspect that is the right answer.

"A boyfriend. That's all he needs to be, not a hero."

"Not a hero," I repeat.

We sit in silence. I count off the seconds in my head. Fifteen. Thirty. Forty-five. The roar of a truck braking on the highway upsets my count at fifty-two. Tires scream. I see the white-blue smoke, the long skid marks. I smell the burning rubber. There's a crash—the guardrail. It's no match for a forty-eight-ton semitrailer veering off the road, out of control. Nearing the edge of the cliff, the driver jumps out of the cab. He hits the dirt and rolls as the truck flies off the edge of the cliff, hanging in the air for a second before plunging down into the rocks and trees below. The giant sounds of destruction shrink and shrink and shrink until there is silence. Someone else witnessing the accident might think it's over. It's not over. I count backwards from three, then cover my ears. *BOOM!* The explosion comes through the ground, up through my feet. It shakes the mountains. It blackens the sky. It pulses in my head like a—

"Boyfriend," says Justine.

I take my hands away from my ears, wipe my nose on my sleeve, sneak a look at my sister. She is staring ahead, through the windshield and out to where the road gets swallowed by the mountains. Whatever emotions she is feeling, I don't immediately recognize them. Her face is somehow smaller, duller, like a camping lantern with the flame turned down. It doesn't even really belong to Justine. I take a deep breath and ask an appropriate question. "Can I do something to help?"

"Wanna drive?"

"What?"

"Kidding." She blinks twice and lets her head flop forward. "Thanks for the offer, Pez. I'll be okay."

She lifts her head and turns. She pulls the rubber band on her wrist and releases so it whips her skin. I don't like it when she does that, but it seems to be part of her routine. Her face loosens up and she smiles. It's not a proper smile, though—it doesn't show any teeth. Justine had that face a lot when we were in school. Whenever Dad saw it, he would say, *Lost your dentures, tree frog?* or *That's your grin-and-bury-it look, tree frog.* She points at the seismometer in my lap.

"I just had a little rumble, that's all," she says. "Take more than that to shake our happy holiday."

I nod because I know Justine would like me to agree with her, but I don't really believe what she says. She is not happy. And I don't think she was joking when she said she would like me to drive. But I can't drive. One lesson per year is not enough.

Perry Richter saves the day.

That is the future.

But not today.

As we leave the small parking lot and accelerate back onto the Coquihalla Highway, I put the seismometer on the floor, holding it between my feet. I will keep it there from now on.

·············●············

THERE ARE NO OTHER RUMBLES for the remaining 161 kilometers of our journey. There are only interesting and beautiful sights for us to see. In my head, I make a separate list for each. By the time we reach the *Peachland Welcomes You* and *Historic Peachland* signs, they are as follows:

<u>Interesting</u>
The abandoned Coquihalla Highway tollbooth
Signs for putting chains on your tires (they don't spell
it *tyres* here) in winter
Overhead bridges that make sure moose and deer and
bears are safe crossing the highway
Fences that make sure the animals use the
overhead bridges
The change from forest mountains to desert hills

Large sections of forest that have died and gone brown
because of a pest called the pine beetle

<u>Beautiful</u>

The snow on the tips of the mountains beside the
Coquihalla Highway

A tiny waterfall running down the side of one of
the mountains

The jade color of the Coquihalla River

A hawk that flew in the sky above our car when we
turned onto Highway 97C

An orange Lamborghini that raced past our car at the
Okanagan Highway turnoff

The final part of the trip—down the long road that
runs beside Okanagan Lake and flattens at the town of
Peachland—could make it onto both lists. The lake is
more like an ocean, calm and blue and reaching for the
horizon. The whole town is positioned on the hillside
to the right; rows of houses overlook the water, no one
missing out on the scenery. It's like a movie theater—
whether you're front row or at the back, everyone has
a good seat for the show. And the movie doesn't have
the thrills and spills of *Rumble in the Bronx* or *Shanghai
Knights*. Just three sailboats and a water-skier and quite
a few swimmers and several people riding Jet Skis.

But it does have Ogopogo, a mystery better than any movie because it is real and not fiction.

"Wow," says Justine. "Never seen anything like this."

"Wow," I repeat.

We find our rental house—it is halfway up the hill, on Beatrice Road. It belongs to a stranger—*Friend of a friend, with maybe another friend thrown in there as well* is what Justine told me. She said the friend's friend's friend travels to Las Vegas at this time every year to earn her children's inheritance and escape the tourists. She showed me photos of the house, outside and in, so I would be prepared. Looking around it now, I'm glad she did. Almost everything is where I expect it to be—kitchen, bedrooms, toilet, the downstairs room with gym equipment, the big glass doors. It doesn't feel like home—that makes me slightly anxious—but it doesn't feel incorrect either. I don't see myself as a burglar or a trespasser or a squatter like the one they kicked out of our neighbor Mrs. McGuire's house after she died of a stroke. This is good practice for Fair Go.

After we've brought the bags in, Justine wipes her brow and puts her hands on her hips. "I need to go shopping," she says. "Gotta grab some groceries and some of your stuff so you don't fade away, Cap'n Ahab."

Justine has called me Captain Ahab before. She's explained the joke to me several times (and I tried to read a few chapters of *Moby Dick*), but I still don't find it funny. I think it's a bit stupid. Captain Ahab and I are nothing alike. He had a wooden leg; I have two regular legs. We also have completely different occupations—he was captain of a boat called the *Pequod*; I am a senior washologist at Troy's Car Care. One way we are similar is that he was an orphan and I am sort of an orphan because Mum left and Dad died. Justine claims the joke is good because both of us are obsessed with mythical beasts of the sea. Although that's true, I still don't think it's choice material. Ahab chased the great white whale because he wanted to harpoon it, as revenge for giving him a disability. Killing Moby Dick was the only thing he was interested in—he was obsessed. I have lots of interests—earthquakes, Jackie Chan movies, washing cars. And if I found Ogopogo in Okanagan Lake I might video it or take a photo of it, but there is no way in the world I would ever want to kill it, even if it hurt me. Killing something because you were injured by it and now you're afraid of it and you don't understand it—that's not being strong. That's being a coward. That's pathetic.

"You go," I say to Justine, looking at her knees instead of her face. "I'll stay here."

"Are you sure?"

"Yes."

"Positive?"

"Like an electric eel." Now, *that's* a funny joke.

"You won't get stressed out?"

"It's good practice for Fair Go."

Justine waits a few seconds, then shrugs her shoulders. "Okay. Here's my number—call me if you need me. Oh, and if the house phone rings, don't pick up. Let the answering machine get it. Don't listen to the message, either—that would be rude."

"What if it's you?"

"It won't be."

"What if it's Ogopogo?"

"That's different. Tell him we'll see him tomorrow, maybe the day after. We'll have tea and scones."

··········●··········

I AM READY TO BE INDEPENDENT for a little while.

My wish is to do some important house chores—Justine will be pleased if I complete a responsible job or two—but there's nothing for me to do. The kitchen sink is clear. The dishwasher is empty. The garbage bins all have new bags. The toilets all have unused rolls. Apart from a small pile of pebbles at the end of the driveway, there's no dust or dirt to be seen. Everything is neat and tidy and in its rightful place.

Usually, I'm happy when everything is organized like this. After I've cleaned and waxed the cars at Troy's, I always smile when the owner says how pleased they are with my work. And I wave when the sparkling vehicle exits the driveway. Today, the work is done and there is only disappointment. I decide to do a second tour of the house, turning on the light switches as I go. I know this is bad for the environment, but I don't like the dark. Some people with my disability enjoy the dark very much; they find it calming and painless, and it slows their minds down so that thoughts can be put together in order and make sense. Not me—I like the light, just as most normal people do.

I take four deep breaths and return to the lounge room. There is so much wood and glass in this house. I doubt it would stay standing in a 6.0 shake. I walk to the edge of the room and press my face against the sliding door that opens onto a small patio and the view of Okanagan Lake. The glass smells like Windex and newspaper ink. A wind chime suspended above the patio sways and dings. The thought that I'm alone in a stranger's home on the other side of the world sneaks into my head. I block it out by reciting the first-aid action plan and flicking the fingers of my right hand. For extra relief, I head for the main toilet. I take a leak, wiping up the splashes on the seat and pressing the half-flush button when I'm done. At least I can do one good thing for the environment.

I unzip our big suitcase and check my clothes—they're squashed but not wrecked. I consider putting them in the chest of drawers near the mirror, then decide against it. There's a framed photograph on top of the chest: a lady with purple hair, wearing lots of makeup and jewelry, is holding a fluffy dog up close to her face. The writing in the corner of the photo says *Janet Beedle 2008*. Is the lady Janet Beedle? Or is it the dog? Maybe the lady is Janet and the dog is Beedle. Or perhaps Janet Beedle is the photographer and the lady's name is Esmeralda and the dog is called Butch. Whatever the story, I know there will be other clothes in the drawers. And putting my T-shirts and shorts and boardies and socks and especially my underwear (or Reg Grundies, as Dad called them) on top of someone else's possessions makes me uncomfortable.

Opening the luggage, I have an idea. If I can't show responsibility, maybe I can show maturity and sophistication by doing something outside my comfort zone. I hunt through the carry-on and pull out the diary Dad wrote for Justine and the book titled *Robinson Crusoe*. Which one to read? It's an easy decision. I would never read the diary Dad wrote for my sister without her permission— that is being a stickybeak and not respecting others' private property. It would be different if it were a diary

Dad wrote for me. As Jus has told me many times, the photo book was Dad's gift to me because I was always a visual learner. In any case, I am familiar with the diary already. Justine sometimes reads bits of it to me, mostly before bed or if I've had a bad turn at home. One time, she read it when the power had gone out because of an evening thunderstorm. She also reads it to me when I ask a question about Dad, or if I've been looking in an old photo album from our Rainbow Beach holidays. She says only the "good time" parts of the diary are for my ears. She's never read the same part twice, so I think there must be more good times than bad.

I put the diary on the bed and return to the living room with *Robinson Crusoe*. The cover is okay—it has the title and a picture of footprints on a patch of sand. It's completely flat though. I like covers with raised bits, when the lettering is bumpy. Running my hand over them, I can pretend I have a different disability—blindness—and I am using braille language.

I open *Robinson Crusoe* to page one and begin to read. It's not easy; the sentences are strange and don't make much sense. A feeling of frustration rises up through my body, like when I tried the monkey bars in second grade and the bars were too far apart and slippery for me to make it all the way across. I don't want to give up though. Justine needs to see that I can show maturity and sophistication by doing something outside my comfort zone. I turn to page 128 and the chapter named "A Cave Retreat." It's better than the earlier chapters—not great but better. There is a part about cannibals and another where Mr. Crusoe discovers a collection of human bones on the beach. It also mentions a human footprint on the sand. I like this because it is an unsolved mystery similar to Ogopogo. And it makes the cover meaningful and not just a dumb picture like some of Jus's other books have on the front.

I reach page 133—the part where Mr. Crusoe is making plans to hide in the trees and shoot the cannibals. I glance out the window. There's a mushroom-shaped tree in the front yard.

"Hide there," I tell him.

Mr. Crusoe follows my advice. He tiptoes across the brown-and-green grass, ducks under the low branches and then crouches down on one knee behind the trunk. Instead of an ancient gun, he's holding a set of nunchuks in his right hand. I'd like to ask him where he found them on his island, but there's no time. The cannibals are coming up the driveway. There are seven of them. Six carry a picnic item—basket, umbrella, tablecloth, fold-up chairs. The seventh has a human body slumped over his shoulder. It's difficult to be absolutely sure who it is, but the overalls and the wristbands and the backward cap and the fact we're in Canada are pretty strong clues.

Justin Bieber.

No lie. The cannibals are planning a Justin Bieber barbecue. A Biebercue.

"He makes bad music," I say to Mr. Crusoe. "But that doesn't mean he should be eaten." I nod my head, and Crusoe jumps out from behind the tree, nunchuks flying. He knocks the front two cannibals down, spilling blood and teeth and plastic cutlery all over the ground. Then he wraps the nunchuks around the neck of cannibal number three and uses him as a shield while roundhouse kicking the remaining trio. Within ten seconds the fight is over. The only cannibal left standing is the Bieber carrier. He is not prepared to go down as easily as his friends. He shifts Bieber off his shoulder and to the front. Then he lifts the teen's forearm up to his smiling, drooling mouth, ready to munch on its meager meat. Mr. Crusoe slowly spins the nunchuks around his waist. Seconds tick. The air is still. The battle has reached a standoff. Castaway and cannibal turn to me, waiting for instructions on what happens next.

I tuck *Robinson Crusoe* under my arm and applaud so they will—

"Having another go at reading a classic, Pez?" says Justine.

I lower my hands, pivot away from the window and face my sister. I perform three big nods to let her know I have been reading and not just creating ridiculous martial arts movies out of classic books. She places two bags of shopping on the counter.

"What do you think so far?"

"It's difficult. It's better than *Moby Dick*."

I'm not joking, but Justine laughs hard. She wipes her eye with her pinkie and begins stacking groceries in the cupboard and the fridge. "If you're into it, keep it for a bit," she says. "I've got my dreams to fill out the blanks in the story."

That last sentence about dreams—I don't understand what that's about. Anyway, I am happy. I did something outside my comfort zone and showed Jus I can be mature and sophisticated. And because I read *Robinson Crusoe* instead of doing chores, my sister showed me something much better than her pleased face—her proud face.

I like that one a lot.

........•••••••........

AT 7:47 PM, THE PHONE RINGS.

"I got it," says Justine, jumping up from the couch. She doesn't answer straight away. She takes the cordless phone from its cradle and jogs into the bedroom, shutting the door behind her. I hear a beep and then she begins to speak. Her voice is low and her conversation is murmurs rather than clear words and sentences. I could probably hear what she was saying if I moved closer, if I maybe held a drinking glass between my ear and the door like I've seen in movies. Eavesdropping is rude, though. So I stare at the TV and try to concentrate on the show we were watching about an entire Canadian town that goes on a diet together.

The waiting hurts. My heart is knocking against the front of my rib cage. I feel hair standing on the back of my neck. Is it Marc phoning again? Must be. Who else would call? I suppose it could be Janet Beedle or maybe a friend of Janet Beedle. But Justine would have got off the phone quickly if it was a stranger. It must be Marc. And that's a problem because Justine said in the Cobalt that his previous call was only a little rumble. Is this a big rumble?

After leaving the toilet on Highway 5, I was prepared for the rest of the drive because the seismometer was with me; I could sense difficulties on the ground and maybe be warned before they started. But when we got here, everything was calm and easy and Jus seemed like she'd forgotten about Marc acting like a hero instead of being a boyfriend. So I left the seismometer in the bedroom. I wish I hadn't been so stupid.

The conversation has reached four minutes. I'm still worried, but the situation hasn't gotten worse. In fact, there are good thoughts starting to enter my head now. Justine continues to speak low. If things weren't going well, she would be raising her voice and saying bad words. She might even cry. I am very, very thankful she is not crying—my sister's tears are torture. It's been that way from the time we were kids. It might've been the same when we were babies, too, but I can't remember back that far. When Jus cries, it's like I've been tied down to a stretching rack. But instead of being stretched up and down by my arms and legs, I'm pulled in all directions with every part of my body—hips, knees, face, finger-nails…even my hair. Everything pulls and screams and burns like molten magma, and it doesn't end when Jus stops crying. It stings for a long time after she's settled down and her eyes are dry.

Six minutes. The diet people in the Canadian town are all doing exercises and giving each other high fives that make the skin on their flabby arms wobble. I hope someone on the show knows CPR. In the bedroom, nothing has changed. The conversation continues and the atmosphere is still calm.

Perhaps Marc is acting like a boyfriend now. It is right that Justine falls in love and has an excellent boyfriend—one that she will move in with and marry and call her soul mate (which means the one person in the world you are meant to be together with, sharing interests, having sex and arguing about things). Is Marc my sister's soul mate? Maybe. She says he is very sweet and romantic and quite handsome and an excellent kisser. She has called him a "great guy" and a "good catch." I've also heard her call him names like "doofus" and "try-hard." She's said three times he *could do with a little less Bingley and a little more Darcy*, which I don't understand, but I know it has something to do with the books she likes to read. I think Marc is a good guy, even though he talks too loud and he knows nothing about earthquakes and his aftershave sometimes makes me throw up a little in my mouth. I think he could be Justine's soulmate. But what I think is not important. It's only important what Justine thinks.

A beep sounds in the bedroom, followed by footsteps on the carpet. I stare ahead at the TV, where an obese woman with a mullet is crying on a treadmill, but I'm really watching the bedroom door open, out of the corner of my eye. Justine emerges, tapping the phone against the palm of her left hand and looking spaced out. She replaces the phone, then sits in the armchair opposite the couch where I am seated. Onscreen, the woman has stopped blubbering and is saying, "I need to do this for my kids."

"That was Marc, yes?" I ask.

Justine looks at me. The focus is back in her eyes. Her brows have jumped up high on her forehead. "What? No, it wasn't Marc, Perry. For his sake, I'm glad it wasn't."

Not Marc?

Not Marc.

Not.

Marc.

The answer is slippery, difficult to grasp, like a soapy sponge at Troy's.

"Are you sure?" I ask.

"Quite sure."

"Okay. Was it someone else from Australia, then?"

"No."

"Was it someone from Canada?"

"Perry—"

"Do you have friends in Canada?"

"Is this Twenty Questions, mate?"

I bow my head and start reading the names of the buttons on the remote control. She takes a deep breath, then swallows the saliva in her mouth.

"I was having a conversation with…my pen pal. I have a Canadian pen pal. You know what that is, don't you?"

I nod. In eighth grade my class wrote to pen pals in Japan. The name of my pen pal was Akiko Suzuki. In my letter, I wrote that the city of Kobe had experienced the Great Hanshin earthquake on Tuesday, January 17, 1995.

It was a 6.8 on the moment magnitude scale and the tremors lasted for twenty seconds. Approximately 6,434 people died, and more than three-quarters of them were from Kobe. I also mentioned that it was not as bad as the Great Kantō earthquake in 1923, which killed 140,000 people. I never received a reply.

"She lives in Vancouver—"

"A 'she'! She's a woman!"

"Yes, Perry, she's a woman. She would like to meet up with us when we come back from Seattle."

"What's her name?"

"That's not something you need to know."

"I do need to know. I get nervous being introduced to strangers. If I know her name, she won't be as much of a stranger and I won't be as nervous."

"It's not something you need to know *right now*."

"Later?"

"Yes, later."

"When?"

Justine takes a deep breath. "When the time is right, Pez."

"I get nervous being introduced to strangers. If I know her name, she won't be as much of a stranger and I won't be as nerv—"

"Okay, okay. Let's say on the drive back from Seattle. How's that?"

I think it over for eleven seconds. "Okay."

"Are you sure?"

"Yes."

"You're not going to ask me about it every half hour for the next few days?"

"No."

"You can handle the suspense?"

"I've got Ogopogo to keep my mind busy," I say. "And I can think about the visit to Bruce Lee's grave in Seattle too."

"Okay. Good."

I can see Justine feels calmer now. The muscles in her jaw are soft again. The flush in her cheeks is changing from red to pink. She walks to the breakfast counter and pulls a bottle out of a brown paper bag.

"Speaking of your sea monster, I managed to find where he lives."

I am confused until she places the bottle in my hands and points to the label. There's a small painting of some land with trees and surrounding water and a mountain in the background. The text in the center says:

Ogopogo's Lair Pinot Grigio

"Mystery solved," says Justine. "He hangs out in a bottle of white."

I begin to giggle because my sister is giggling. Then it becomes a full-on laugh because I get an image in my brain of the creature in a lake full of wine, swimming and hiccupping and singing "Last Train to Gaythorne" the way Dad used to when he'd had a few "ten-ounce sandwiches."

And the uncomfortable idea of meeting a stranger in Vancouver becomes separate and harmless, like a spider trapped in a glass jar.

........●........

THE BEST DAY SO FAR of our North American adventure has arrived. I am wearing boardies and a T-shirt. I've put on my floppy hat and sunscreen. My backpack has snacks and water and the *Rush Hour* DVD and my stuffed Ogopogo. I have Justine's digital camera, which also shoots video.

It was difficult waiting for today. Yesterday did not go as quickly as I would've liked. The night before, Justine put together a map of all the different Ogopogo fakes—statues and fountains and paintings and plaques—that people have done for tourists. After breakfast we drove to Kelowna to see them all.

First, we saw a fountain in a park. The monster was greenish-brown, had the head/two humps/tail, and its snout looked like it belonged to a hippopotamus. Water shot out of its ears and head. I doubt this is accurate or true to life. Next, we saw a giant painting that someone had done on the side of a building. It was probably the best and most interesting art of the day. The creature was drawn as a good mix of dinosaur and sea serpent, and the picture showed it chewing on plants beneath the surface of the lake. In the afternoon we went to a tiny beach in Kelowna, close to the bridge crossing Okanagan Lake. At the children's water park, there were two "play" statues—I didn't like them. One was a large green head with climbing ropes all over it and a long red tongue hanging from its mouth. I don't know what the artist was thinking, but to me it was gross. You didn't have to use much imagination to see the tongue as a trail of blood, or to think hunters had cut the head off Ogopogo's dead body and left it there for the seagulls. The other statue wasn't gross—it was just a bit blah. The body was okay, the same as the fountain—head/two humps/tail—but the face looked like it belonged to a King Charles spaniel. And the big chunky tongue was something you would see in the meat section of a grocery store rather than any proper book on Ogopogo.

When we came back to the Janet Beedle Peachland house, Justine asked me if I had enjoyed the day. I didn't want to say it was meh, so I told her it had made me more excited for our boat tour of the lake tomorrow. And now the next day is here. I'm trying to be calm and collected. I'm squeezing my fists tight and rolling my shoulders, feeling the weight of the backpack. The data this morning was off the charts. I don't have the seismometer here with me for the boat ride, but I know it would still be showing instability. I can feel it in my feet. It's as if I'm walking fast on an asphalt road in summer and it's getting hotter and hotter with each step. No lie, something is set to happen.

Something good, I reckon.

••••••••••●••••••••••

THE BOAT FOR OUR TOUR—THE *Kathleen Rita,* according to the fancy writing on the bow—looks old and has peeling paint. The captain is standing on the dock as we approach, his back to us, head forward. He turns when he hears our footsteps, but his head remains down. He's reading a magazine. We stop a meter in front of him and wait for him to look up, but he keeps reading. Ten seconds go by. I grab the three fingers of Justine's right hand and squeeze. I was uneasy drawing near, but now I'm a little bit annoyed. He's ignoring us! What gives?! Justine squeezes back and it helps take my mind off the man's bad manners. I think about the soft, fluffy, yellow belly of the Ogopogo stuffed toy in my backpack.

"Hi. You wouldn't happen to be Clinton Muckler?" asks Jus.

The man closes the magazine and holds it in front of his belt buckle. The title of the magazine is *Soap Opera Weekly*. The subheadings are *3 Huge Secrets Exposed!* and *Baby Revealed!* and *Shocking Seduction!* The exclamation points are like cymbal clashes in my brain. More seconds pass.

"I am, ma'am," the man replies, smiling.

Clinton Muckler is large—not fat, just big in all the parts of his body. His teeth are the size of piano keys. He's wearing a cap that has *Boston Bruins* written on it and wraparound sunglasses that help sailors keep the glare out of their eyes. There is a tattoo of an eagle and an anchor and some numbers on his right forearm. A long pink scar shaped like a banana stretches from just under his left knee to the top of his ankle.

"I believe we've booked your services, yes?" says Justine.

More seconds pass, and Clinton Muckler doesn't say anything. He rolls his head from side to side and makes grunting noises in his throat. This is bad behavior. To not answer someone when they've asked you a question very nicely—that's *so* inappropriate. Why would he do this?

What is his reason? Is he trying to make us scared? Angry? Is this his stupid idea of fun? If it is, then he is a bad guy—the sort of person Dad would've called a "rolled-gold asshole."

And, suddenly, I'm thinking the best day so far of our North American adventure could become the worst. It's not fair that rude individuals can spoil things like that. I realize no one can force you to feel things, good or bad. You are responsible for the actions of your hands and the words from your mouth and the feelings in your heart. Dad used to tell me: *If you go through life finding fault in others, you'll end up in a world of one.* He said we need the people around us—warts and all—and I understand this much better now that I'm older.

At Fair Go I will be on my own, but I will need help with some of the tasks—cooking and sewing and maintenance around my place and the farming jobs they get all residents to do. And the help I need will come from the people around me. But Fair Go is not the same as planet Earth, and not all people are helpers. Some are rolled-gold assholes. They kick your basketball away in the school playground or they move when you sit next to them on the train or they drop cigarettes into your sponge bucket at the car wash or they call you a spaz and a retard. It's very difficult to be responsible and pretend bad people's faults are invisible. And if you have more bad people around you than good, you might even begin to think a world of one is okay.

I am ready to say we can find another boat to hire. I take a tighter hold of Justine's fingers. Then Mr. Muckler speaks.

"Yes, you on board my *Kathleen Rita* for the day, Ms. Richter. Very nice to meet you. And this strong fella must be Perry."

He holds out his hand. My right hand keeps gripping the strap of my backpack. After a while he lowers his hand. I can see in my peripheral vision that Justine is giving me a gruff look.

"Sorry about that," she says, keeping her eyes locked on me. "Perry's not great with introductions. He has a brain condition that can cause him to feel anxious or upset in different places and circumstances. He has trouble with people—mixing with them and communicating with them—and it sometimes results in inappropriate behaviors. I appreciate your understanding and patience."

Often, when Justine tells people the spiel, they say something quickly afterward like *I'm so sorry* or *That's so sad* or *I didn't realize*. Not Clinton Muckler. There's another long pause. More grunting noises come from his throat. He takes off his sunglasses and hangs them on the front of his collar.

"Perry, your sister's email said you got a real interest in Ogopogo."

I know he's looking to make eye contact, but I don't want to. I focus on his tattoo. "That is correct."

"I bet you know a lot about him."

"Yes, I do. I have done a lot of research."

"I bet you have, I bet you have…And you're from Australia, huh?"

"Yes."

"I bet you're one of the few Aussies who's heard about Ogopogo, huh?"

I don't want to have a conversation with a rude individual, even if Ogopogo is the subject. Jus is still giving me the hairy eyeball, though. I stiffen and imagine I am washing away his tattoo with my car-wash sponge.

"I'm guessin' you know some of the famous sightings," says Muckler after another round of grunts. "The places on the lake we're gonna see—you prob'ly be able to tell me what happened before I can flap my gums. But there's a few sightin's you don' know about." He runs his tongue over his bottom lip and leans closer. "Mine."

"Yours?"

"Yessir."

"You've seen Ogopogo."

"Yessir. More than a few times, in actual fact."

I look at Jus. The tough face is gone, replaced by one I can't easily read. Her eyes are bugged and her eyebrows are arched upward. Her lips are pulled into a straight line, like a stretched elastic band. She's not looking at Clinton Muckler, the person who has the surprising information. She's still staring at me.

"You don' believe me, Perry?" he says, directing his gaze toward the lake. "You wouldn' be alone in thinkin' that. Lotta people in these parts figure I might be a bit...left field with what I seen. A little off base with my perception. Don' get me wrong—they believe I seen somethin'. Current perhaps. Debris. Wake from a Jet Ski passed by. But the monster? The legendary beast? Nah, couldn't *really* be that. Not when the eyes belong to a brain-fried vet."

I can't see my own face, but I'm sure it has a shocked look. "Brain-fried...You are...? Does that mean you are disabled?"

Clinton Muckler grunts and rubs his neck. He takes off the Boston Bruins cap, revealing a grayed crew cut. There is a scar on his head—not banana shaped like the one on his leg, but zigzagged like a traced outline of a tectonic plate slip. A wound like that would've used all of the bandages in my first-aid kit at home.

"Got m'self a bad blow during the first Gulf War. Scalped me and then some. Bad business. Came home to a medical discharge, pension. After I'd rehabbed, I figured I'd do some adventurin' with the money. I could still drive okay so long as I wasn't actin' like Dale Earnhardt and I didn't drive at night. So I got m'self a Winnebago and traveled 'round."

He stops for a bit, poking his chin out. I get a picture in my mind of words caught in his throat like fish bones.

"First my home state, Idaho," he continues. "Then back and forth cross the States, then up into Canada. When I got to the Okanagan, I stayed put. Fell in love with the place. The people, the lake, the desert hills. I figured the desert owed me a little somethin' after what happened in Iraq. An' I fell in love with Ogopogo. The real beast, but also the idea of him too." He laughs and runs his hand over his tattoo, as if he's rubbing sunscreen into it. "So, now me and *Kathleen Rita* putter up an' down the lake, keepin' the good ol' boy company. It's a good life. Slow an' reality-free. The way I need it to be."

A second image pops into my head—one in which Clinton Muckler is working at Troy's Car Care. His bucket of water has many cigarettes floating on the surface. Each cigarette has my name printed on it. I dig my fingernails into my thigh and the image fades.

He turns back and smiles at Jus, then at me. "You have trouble with people—mixin' with them and communic-atin' with them? I got that sort o' trouble too, only with words and thoughts. Takes me a little longer to get 'em makin' sense. Mainly goin' in, sometimes comin' out."

He moves a bit closer. I smell bacon and turpentine. "But I'll swear to the good Lord on high, there's nothin' wrong with my eyes. How 'bout yours, Perry?"

"My eyesight is excellent."

"I bet it is. I bet you see things real good."

He puts his cap back on his head and extends his arm toward the *Kathleen Rita*. Instead of stepping onto the boat, I take Clinton Muckler's outstretched hand and pump it three times. I thought he was a rolled-gold asshole. I didn't say it out loud though—I only thought it. But apologizing is still the right thing to do.

"I believe you've seen Ogopogo. And I'm sorry I didn't shake your hand before."

Clinton Muckler grunts, nods. Although I'm not familiar with reading his face, I'm pretty sure his look means he understands.

...........●●●...........

MY SISTER KNOWS I LIKE to give expert ear bashings about Ogopogo. Today, for eight hours, it is my ear being bashed. We travel partway up the 135-kilometer lake, seeing places where the creature has been spotted. It's exciting building a catalog of pictures in my mind and on Justine's digital camera. I snap all the stops:

the place of the first recorded sighting by a white person—Mrs. Susan Allison—in 1872; the path of the Miller and Marten couples' motorboat, which the monster followed for three minutes in 1959; the 2004 location of John Casorso's houseboat when it was shaken up by a strange disturbance, leading to fifteen minutes of video footage and an article in the local newspaper.

Clinton Muckler is an excellent guide, adding interesting information to the facts I have learned through my own research. He talks about the famous 1978 eyewitness account of a man named Bill Steciuk. (I am familiar with his website and his title of "Legend Hunter." I also know he is trying to gain proof of the monster with modern equipment such as sonar and thermal imaging.) Clinton says the sighting was actually shared by twenty other motorists who, like Mr. Steciuk, had stopped on the west side of the Kelowna Bridge. He also mentions that the crowd watched the monster swimming around for nearly one minute.

Just as interesting as the extra information is its effect on Clinton Muckler. He speaks clearly and at an even pace. There are very few grunts or long pauses. He answers questions without needing to concentrate. Expert ear-bashing has the same effect on him as it does on me—it makes us calm and comfortable. It helps lessen the brain hassles in activities like going to the shopping center or standing in line at a restaurant or being a passenger on a crowded bus. Late in the day, Clinton Muckler talks about his own close encounters. No lie, he's had *seventeen* sightings in all, each one in and around Rattlesnake Island, visible to the town of Peachland. It is believed that Ogopogo lives in the Squally Point caves below our boat.

"Have you ever filmed or photographed any of them?" asks Jus.

"Nope," Clinton replies, shrugging his shoulders. "I know what I know. Don' need a video to tell me that. Don' need to show anythin' to the rest o' the world either. What other people think is up to them." He turns to me and points to the camera hanging over my wrist. "How 'bout you, Perry? You wanna capture the beast on film? Become a big-time celebrity, like the ones I see in *Soap Opera Weekly*?"

The question is unexpected, and the answer is not simple. Immediately, my heart jumps and my palms begin to sweat. I scrunch fists for a few seconds, curl toes inside my runners.

"Before my father died," I say, "I told him I would take care of Justine. I promised I would do something amazing one day so he wouldn't have to worry about us. I have a few ideas. One is to take the first proper photograph of the Loch Ness Monster and sell it to Yahoo!

When I return home to Brisbane, I am going to live in the Fair Go Community Village, so I don't think we'll be going to Scotland anytime soon."

"I see. So, Ogopogo would be just as good, yeah?"

"He's not as well known, but I think proof of his existence would be worth a lot of money."

Clinton Muckler nods. He leans against the side rail of the *Kathleen Rita* and scratches his unshaven chin. "If you don' mind me askin'...When did your daddy pass?"

I don't mind. The answer is a date—an easy fact to recall. And if I picture it circled on a calendar, I don't think so much about Dad being sick in bed or crying at night or the funeral where his body was burned to ashes and scattered over Rainbow Beach. "Twenty-ninth of September, 2008."

"Just before our eighteenth birthdays," adds Justine.

The quiver in her voice is a light slap across my face. She takes my hand, and I release the breath held in my chest.

Clinton Muckler grunts for the first time in a long time. He gives a small flick of his head, like he's trying to shoo a fly that's landed on his nose. "I'm real sorry for your loss."

He takes off his sunglasses, places them in a case lying next to the steering wheel.

"Takin' care of your sister—that's a real good reason to wanna prove Ogopogo's real. Almost makes me hope the good ol' boy'll come up into the light an' make it happen."

·············●●·············

THE GOOD OL' BOY NEVER MADE it happen.

When we return to the dock, I have taken eighty-one photographs. None of them contains Canada's most famous mythical sea animal.

"You disappointed?" asks Justine, holding my shoulders. I answered this already. Clinton Muckler asked the question when we stepped back onto the dock, just after he shook my hand and just before he started *Kathleen Rita*'s engine and motored away. I told him no. I was prepared to give an explanation, but he didn't ask for one.

He grunted, wiped his forehead, said he was glad. "Best customers I ever had shouldn' go away feelin' cheated," he added.

Justine wants an explanation though. I close my eyelids to slits so that her face is blurry. "Ogopogo was close the whole time," I say. "I knew he was there, near the surface. Maybe even peeking out of the lake every now and then, just to see what we were doing. He is a curious creature. But he is also smart." A ladybug lands on the collar of Jus's shirt. I am thankful—I can look at it but still appear focused. "If I'd seen him, it would've been because he let me. Because he had a good reason for me to see him."

"Ogopogo was there?"

"Yes."

"You felt it."

"Yes."

Justine glances at the camera hanging from my wrist. "So if Ogopogo had let you see him, if he had a good reason…Would you have taken a picture?"

I give three big shakes of the head. "I would've just watched. No lie. I would've told him he was safe with me." I take my sister's wrists, lower her arms down to her sides and grab hold of the middle, ring and pinkie fingers of her right hand. "I'll do something else amazing."

Justine scans my face, studying every different part, as if she's inspecting a car-detailing job. "You're already amazing," she says.

"Shut the hell up!" I reply.

"No. You're amazing!"

"Shut the hell up!"

"Okay, then. You're a dickhead!"

"Shut the hell up!"

We perform Dad's pity laugh—the one he said he stole from George McFly in *Back to the Future*—then have a proper giggle. When it's done, Jus hugs me. I am pleased to find her hair smells like tea-tree oil even though we are far from home. Her voice is muffled by my shoulder. "What you said about taking care of me—that was very sweet."

"I meant it."

"Yes. You did." She gives me a hard squeeze, then steps back, her hands holding mine. "You want a couple more minutes at the water before we head back?"

"Yes."

"Okay. I'll wait at that bench over there."

She walks off and I turn to view Ogopogo's back-yard one final time. The colors have changed since this morning. Everything is darker, as if the water has soaked into the landscape. Homing in on Rattlesnake Island, I think about the modern equipment being used in searches—the thermal imaging and the Remote Operating Vehicle and the sonar. Will the people chasing Ogopogo ever get proof? Will they ever believe what Clinton Muckler already knows? What *I* know? It's doubtful. The chasers are like Captain Ahab—they're not doing it for the right reasons. And even if they found the creature and caught him in a net and brought him onto land and put him in a zoo, and the story was seen on

TV and the Internet and then they made a movie called *Ogopogo Is All Up in Your Face*—even if all that happened, I think there would still be people who would say it was a lie because they didn't understand and were afraid.

My imagination is taking over. I am actually hearing a sonar sound: *beep-beep…beep-beep…beep-beep… BEEP*. And there's a voice that follows the end of the beeps. An upset voice. I turn my head and realize it's not my imagination and it isn't sonar.

··········●··········

"HOW MANY TIMES DO WE have to have this conversation? Seriously, I can't believe we're doing this again… AAAARGH!"

Her shout is a punch on the jaw, a kick to the guts. She stomps the ground with her right foot. The earth shifts.

"You know something bad is going to happen, do you? How do you know, Marc? Tell me…Oh, you just *know*, do you? You've got her all figured out—"

Cracks.

"No, you're *not* protecting me. This is all about *you*, Marc. You and this *ridiculous* don't-mess-with-my-woman thing you've got going on…"

My legs give and I tip forward, hand holding my stomach. Splotches appear in front of my eyes, like wasted bugs on a windshield. Justine's pained voice keeps coming, piling onto my neck and shoulders, buckling my knees.

"You know what? This is too much for me to handle right now. It really is. This trip, the appointment, Perry's move when we get back—I don't need the extra aggravation. I'm sorry…"

Her words are flying objects now, random and dangerous. They are spears hurled into my brain. They are the crazy legs of evil John attacking at will, and I am Jackie Chan, drunk and helpless and suffering. I wonder if they'll ever end. I don't wonder for long.

"What am I saying? I'm saying if you *love* me, Marc, you'll leave me alone. That's what I need…How long? For the rest of this trip…When we get back? Right now, I have no clue. I really don't. All I know is this cannot continue. We need a break, starting now…"

I don't want to hear this. But it was spoken, so it can't be taken back. Justine and Marc—it's over. No more. He is gone and my sister is by herself. She is alone, without a soul mate.

The consequences rush toward me like a death squad of ninjas, throwing grenades at my head.

BANG!

If she holds on to you…
BANG!
…she won't let go.
BANG!
It's not fair to her.
BANG!
She would never be free.

Another beep. My sister's crying is quiet. She's trying to stop it from coming out, trying to catch it in her belly and in her throat. She can't hide it. Not from me. Her shaky breaths and tiny sobs grip me, rip me. Pain stretches every cell in my body. I am splitting into two and into four and into eight. I am a jigsaw puzzle. Any second now I will be caught by the wind and scattered across the ground. I wait and wait. I stay on all fours. Something is holding me in place, stopping me from falling through the earth. Something powerful. My body is seismic, but I can lift my head and focus on the lake.

Ogopogo is everything I imagined. His body is a perfect prehistoric design—smooth and sleek, shinier than a brand-new quarter. He moves quickly and easily, dipping and rolling without disturbing the surface. At some angles, his scaly skin changes to the same blue-green of the lake, making him seem more like a ghost than a living animal. Four times, he looks up at the cloudless sky and its fading light. Does he want to fly like the brown hawk high above? Then he turns toward me. The air is still. The distance between us is a stone's throw.

I know Jus is still upset, but that knowledge is wrapped in a bubble floating over my head. The pain is now outside my body. Ogopogo watches, his horselike head swaying. His face is lined and scarred; his gray eyes are even. I think he is calm. I think he trusts me. After twenty seconds, maybe thirty, he lifts higher out of the water, as if obeying a command to stand and salute. He shudders and flicks his huge spike of a tail. A long rope of spray drenches the dock. Several fat droplets hit the ground in front of me. Ignoring the tremor in my hand, I reach forward and touch the wet patches. They feel alive; an electric current runs through them, or maybe the pulses of a tsunami from a hundred years ago. I lift my fingers and touch my lips and tongue. Tingly threads fill my mouth and throat. They stitch together and spread through my whole body until there is a frosty blanket covering the pain.

I can think now. I can dig the ninjas' shrapnel out of my skin, line them up on the ground, view them as a problem to solve. Almost immediately, the answer rises high and flicks its tail.

Set her free.

Perry Richter saves the day—that is the future.

And the future is now.

No lie.

I look toward Ogopogo one final time, hoping to whisper a thank-you. He is no longer there. The splashes on the dock have dried up. The surface of the lake is a sheet of glass. The hawk still circles above.

Jus's grief is a feather. I fall forward onto my stomach.

........•••••••••........

I START PLANNING DURING OUR journey to Seattle.

Justine doesn't do much other than drive, just as she didn't do much other than watch TV last night. She wears sunglasses all day, even when we're inside. On the road, she keeps the car's satellite radio tuned to the "Nineties on Nine" station. When she does speak, it's a quote from the classics she likes to read:

"It isn't what we say or think that defines us, but what we do."

"Know your own happiness. Want for nothing but patience—or give it a more fascinating name: Call it hope."

"Where people wish to attach, they should always be ignorant...A woman especially, if she have the misfortune of knowing anything, should conceal it as well as she can..."

At the United States border crossing, she sniffles, blows her nose. When the officer asks if she's okay, Justine blames it on allergies. The officer gives a pretend smile and tells us to enjoy our stay. Passing the Tulalip Resort, Justine swears and bangs her hands five times on the steering wheel. Near Seattle's big stadiums—Safeco Field for baseball and CenturyLink Field for football—she pulls off her rubber band and throws it out the window. I don't mind the lack of conversation or social interaction. They're great during an adventure, but this is no longer an adventure. This is a rescue, like the one following the 1993 Los Angeles earthquake, when a street sweeper was pulled out of the collapsed Northridge Center and its six-meter-high pancake stack of a car park.

To set my sister free, I must make her afraid. Not for a week or a day, just for a few hours. It won't be pretty, especially after her freak-out over the swimming note at the Pacifica West Hotel. I can see her reaction. Panic will appear on her face: lines on her forehead, big eyes, color in her cheeks and neck, incisor teeth biting into the bottom lip. Her heart will pound. Her breathing will be shorter, quicker. Her stomach will be full of butterflies. Her mind and her feet will race.

It won't be a simple procedure for me, either. I will be very nervous. Alone in a large American city, wandering streets only seen before on a map, having to talk to total strangers with TV accents. It will unnerve me for sure. But I will find solutions to any problems that come up because I won't have my sister to rely on. I will be Master Disaster, brave and strong.

I have two possible options—the visit to Bruce Lee's grave on Saturday and the visit to Pike Place Fish Market on Sunday. So the next day I do my homework on both, scoping out the locations, listing surrounding landmarks, studying routes to the closest police station. Twice during the evening Jus asks me what I'm up to. I tell her I am investigating the twin tragedies of Bruce Lee's death and his son Brandon Lee's death and the claim by some people that there is a curse on the family name.

"Wonderful subject," she says with a voice I know is sarcastic. "Lives snuffed out just when they were getting started."

She sighs. She's doing that now instead of quoting her classics. A small flutter sometimes appears in her right eyelid. If she were feeling better, she would remember I'm not hardcore into Bruce Lee. I like his movie *Enter the Dragon*, and I like that he was an inspiration for the teenage Jackie Chan when they filmed *Fist of Fury*, and I think his unfortunate death from a cerebral edema is an interesting first-aid mystery. And there is no doubt he was super fit and an amazing martial artist. But there are negative things about Bruce Lee too. He only ever made one good movie. He didn't do movies in English. He didn't make jokes—he wasn't funny in the slightest. In fact, he looked either serious or angry pretty much all the time. Jus knows where I stand on Bruce Lee. If she were feeling better, she would suspect I was researching something else, something I didn't want her to know about.

..............●..............

ON SATURDAY MORNING, DRIVING TO Lakeview Cemetery, I decide I will make my sister afraid during the visit to Pike Place tomorrow. When we arrive at Lot 276—the location of Bruce and Brandon Lee's graves—I know for sure I made the right choice. Looking around Lakeview, a number of factors would've created problems. The crowd is small. The cemetery has a lot of open space, with the headstones providing the only decent cover. And because it is a place of sadness and silence, there is not much noise or activity to be a distraction.

On the way back to the car, Justine asks me what I thought of it. I tell her the graves were very well maintained, the marble shone, and all the flowers were fresh rather than withered. And, no lie, I thought there would be more Asian people present.

"Great. It was a disappointment."

"No, it was different. Quiet and open and not very crowded."

She folds her arms. "I thought you'd prefer it that way?"

I shrug, knowing on this day, nothing could be further from the truth.

·········•·········

"PEZ, I DON'T KNOW IF you understand, because I've been such a downer lately—if you don't, I just want to make absolutely sure—the thing with Marc had nothing to do with you."

Justine is beside me, her arm looped through mine. Her left leg is tucked in beside my right, hip to ankle, as if preparing for a three-legged race. We are at the Pike Place Fish Market, waiting for the men in the orange overalls— the world-famous fish throwers—to be funny and entertaining. The crowd builds with each minute. The area in front of the counter is packed. A section of cobblestoned street behind is also filling up. There is a lot of noise— people talking loudly, laughing, car engines revving and idling, a faraway siren, a whistle, a man shouting about a passage from the Bible. There is plenty of movement too—mostly slow-walking visitors on the street, looking at the different shops and stalls. Some are quicker, like the ponytailed man on a segway and the older couple wearing matching American-flag tracksuits and riding a tandem bike.

"You weren't to blame," says Jus.

"Duh," I reply.

She laughs and squeezes my arm. She is relieved. I am the opposite of relieved. I am counting breaths and trying to keep them evenly spaced. Normally, humming or squeezing my fists or running my hands up and down my thighs would help settle me. But Justine knows they are my calming behaviors, and even though I have good excuses for feeling anxious—the sounds, close strangers, the smells of fish and candle wax and paint—I want her to think I am handling the situation well.

I wish she would let go of my arm.

Justine looks at her watch, makes a sucking noise with her lips. "This show must be kicking off soon, hey?"

"They don't do shows," I reply.

"What's that?"

"I researched Pike Place Fish Market and they don't do set shows, not like a circus or a theme park. They just serve customers. They make people feel good by being excellent servants."

"And through airborne fish."

"Of course. That's what made them well known. That was their mission." I point to the shop logo, which has an orange banner with the words *WORLD FAMOUS* written on it. "They achieved that. They now have a different mission—world peace."

"World peace?"

"Yes. It says so on their website."

"They want to achieve world peace by tossing a few mullet around?"

"I don't think they have mullet. They mainly throw salmon."

One of the orange overalls—a thick man with acne scars and a handlebar mustache—laughs with a lady wearing very large hoop earrings and a purple Washington Huskies sweater. Looking around the crowd and the passersby, I see Huskies clothing everywhere—T-shirts and tank tops and trackpants. One girl has some very short shorts with *WH* printed on the bum. I also notice groups of Washington State Cougars fans wearing red. I wish I had college sport merchandise—it would've been much easier to blend in.

Justine looks at her watch again. "We don't have to stay here long if you don't want to."

I jerk my head, causing my cap to tilt sideways. My breath count starts over.

"You okay?"

"I…I am fine."

"You sure?"

"I am fine, Just Jeans." I give her the widest smile I can manage.

"Okay, Pez, okay. I believe you," she says, patting my forearm. "Keep the teeth fillings to yourself."

There are a number of places I could make a getaway, but the fish market is the best opportunity. It has the crowd, the noise, and there are excellent escape routes and hideouts close by. And it possesses one special way to make sure Justine's focus is elsewhere.

"You're going to buy a fish so you can catch it, aren't you?" I ask.

Jus turns her head and leans back a little. "What…me?"

"Yes."

"I thought the guys who work in the shop did all the throwing and catching."

"No. The customers also do it. Customers like you."

Justine pulls a sour-taste face and rubs the back of her neck with her free hand. "I don't know, Pez. It was hard enough catching a basketball at school, let alone a barramundi."

"You don't have to worry about catching a barramundi, because they don't have any."

"And what the hell are we going to do with the fish when I've caught it? We're driving back to Vancouver this afternoon. Where are we going to store it? In the glove box?"

"We could buy a cooler bag. Or a small cooler."

"Not really the souvenirs I was looking to bring back."

"You wouldn't have to buy it, Justine. I could buy it."

I jerk my head again. This is unexpected. Coolers, glove boxes, Jus's poor catching skills—I hadn't thought about any of these things. And now they're threatening to upset my plan.

I want to sink down, lie on the ground. I can't do it. This is the future, the moment when Perry Richter saves the day. I wriggle out of Justine's grasp, move in front of her and put my hands on her shoulders. She lifts her sunglasses, and I stare directly into her surprised face. The heat is building in my sockets and my sinuses. I say the words *brave* and *strong* in my mind and imagine a fire extinguisher filling my skull with white foam.

"Are you…s-seeing me?" I ask, pushing through a stammer. "I don't want you to think about the problems. I want you to leave them alone so you can take part in this. It's important."

"Why? Why is this so important?"

"Because…because I am not seeing you. I want you to smile and be yourself, Just Jeans."

A small breath catches in Justine's throat. Her mouth tightens, her chin wobbles slightly, then stops. She crosses her arm over her chest, lifts her hand to her shoulder and lays it on mine.

"You're right," she says, her voice low. "You're dead right. I need to get back on track. The Marc Debacle has caused enough grief already."

"You should call it The Demarcle."

Jus bursts out laughing, then pulls me into a weak headlock. When she releases, her face is transformed: normal; open and bright, like a flower that has found the sun.

"Okay, time to catch a fish," she says, pretending to put on a pair of gloves and slapping her hands together. "My best chance at not embarrassing myself might be those swordfish steaks."

She gives me a kiss on the cheek and lets go of my arm. The instant we separate, I feel like a passenger without a seat belt in a speeding car. I edge back a single step. My feet prickle. My heart is a boxer's punching bag. Jus stands at the counter. After thirty seconds or so, she is told by one of the staff that she will be served real soon. I take another step back. The ground doesn't slip; the earth doesn't open. I am steady and solid. The skinniest of the orange overall men talks to my sister, and she points to a display of silver-and-gray fish. The skinny man shouts, "Sockeye salmon!" and the rest of the overalls repeat the shout. Another talk takes place and Justine is escorted behind the counter.

I am on the street.

If she looks for me now, if she finds me putting distance between us, I won't give up. I will remain calm. I will wave. I will give her a thumbs-up. I might even tell a joke: *I'm standing over here so I don't get hit!* But it's not necessary. There is no need to flick my spiked tail. Justine is smiling, laughing, preparing her hands for a fishy catch. She is herself. And she has forgotten about me.

As the crowd counts down, I jog down Pike Place, headed for Pine Street.

My target: the Seattle Police Department's West Precinct.

··········●··········

I MOVE QUICKLY PAST POSTAL ALLEY, toward 1st Avenue. The intersection is busy and there's a wait at the crossing light. I flick my hands, then concentrate on the sound—a rubbery *chid-chid-chid*—and the feeling of blunt needles poking at my wrists and knuckles. My thoughts fight to overcome the urge to peek over my shoulder at the image of Justine's panicked face. The light turns green and I set off like a walker in the Olympics, but without the stupid high arm swing and the equally stupid bum wiggle.

After one hundred strides I feel calmer and less like Jackie Chan escaping to Hong Kong in *Supercop*. My senses are keen. A whiff of popcorn drifts out of an office block. A frizzy-haired busker near a restaurant called Yummy Bowl is playing one of Dad's favorite songs— "Heart of Gold" by Neil Young. The city buses— eight have passed by since my entering Pine Street— are painted green and gold. At the intersection of Pine and 4th Avenue, one of the interesting features from my Google Maps research moves into view: hundreds of different-colored bricks in the road, creating a giant quilt pattern of lines and squiggles and zigzags. I walk along one of the gray brick lines on 4th before hopping over to a red stripe near a fire hydrant. It would feel good to touch the pattern with my hands, to view it from all directions: north, south, east and west. Maybe on the way back from the police station.

Farther along Pine Street, at the site of the Paramount Theater, I stop and look behind me. Pedestrians are wandering the sidewalks. Traffic is cruising the street. Trees are shifting to and fro in the breeze. No running, no shouting voices, no sirens and lights that might ruin the rescue. No sign of my sister.

"The shaking won't last forever, Jus," I murmur.

Thoughts of her losing it are not as stark now. The picture of her tense, desperate face—it's like a reminder note or a shopping list. I can hold it at arm's length and read it without feeling anxious. I can fold it in half and put it in my pocket, keeping it safe until she is set free; when that time comes, I can scrunch it up into a ball and throw it away for good. That time is soon. The distance from 9th Avenue to Virginia Street will require ten minutes, fifteen tops. It won't be long before I see her angry face.

I feel strong as I stride onto 9th. Brave and strong. I am Robinson Crusoe leaving footprints in the sand. I stand straighter, taller. I think about how others might be seeing me. Often, people notice me for the wrong reasons. Perhaps, in these moments of bravery and strength, I am standing out in a good way?

Three girls across the street seem to think so. They're staring, talking behind their hands and giggling. The middle one—blond-haired with tight-fitting clothes and large breasts—blows a kiss at me. Why? I guess she likes the way I look and she's paying me a compliment. If it were me, I would do something different. Many women don't like a blown kiss or a wolf whistle or a pelvic thrust from a stranger. They see it as the man wanting to have sex with them, not understanding they have brains that can think about things other than shopping for shoes, and bodies that can do a lot more than give birth to babies.

"Thank you!" I call out. "That's very nice of you!"

The talking and giggling behind hands continues. Then the blond girl shouts, "Noice! Noice! Hey, put anotha shrimp on the bah-bee, sexy Aussie man!"

I have no idea what she's talking about, except for the last bit. I also have no clue about the age of these girls. Are they eighteen? Are they twenty-eight? It's always so hard to tell. If they're under eighteen, I don't feel comfortable with them calling me sexy. "How old are you?"

"Old enough, Aussie hottie!"

More giggling. The two on either side of the blond share a fist bump. I realize it's my turn to speak, but I don't know what to say. And this is a ridiculous way to have a conversation—shouting over the tops of passing cars, from one side of the street to the other. Luckily, I have a good excuse to move on. "Well, I must get going. I'm walking to the police station and I don't want to be late. Thank you, again. Goodbye."

Before my sentence is finished, the girls have turned away. They walk toward the 9th–Pine intersection, swaying their hips and loudly singing a rap song with a lot of swearwords in the lyrics.

There is a lot of construction happening on the left side of 9th. Several buildings are little more than frames, skeletons waiting for their concrete muscles and their particleboard organs. Cranes stand over their heads. Pallets of bricks lie at their feet. Cyclone fences surround them, making sure people understand the danger in getting too close. It's like a repair job after a quake. That's what I'm doing—a repair job after the tremor Marc brought to Justine. Her heart was damaged and now it needs to be fixed. It will be, once she has been set free. She will fall in love again. Hopefully not months after my move to Fair Go. Weeks would be good, or, even better, days. If I had my seismometer I could maybe get a proper idea of the time.

No lie, I think love is like a Jackie Chan stunt—everything must be right for it to work. Love is a very complicated action scene. Much more complicated than Candice May asking me for a kiss outside the school library in eighth grade. Much more complicated than the drunk waitress at the Normanby Hotel giving me a "groin grope" (that's what Justine called it) on our nineteenth birthdays. Jus has said many times I am handsome. When I was sixteen, she told me I was a ladies' man and I had a look women liked. She wouldn't be surprised if I told her I had a kiss blown my way and I was called sexy by an unknown girl on a Seattle street. But how does she feel about me falling in love? Dating and sex and marriage… Does she believe they will happen for me sometime in the future? I'm not sure I want them to happen.

Love has lots of unspoken words, so much silent communication. Reading and understanding unspoken language is difficult enough at the car wash, let alone in a bar or on a dance floor or in a chat room. And Dad never had another wife or a serious girlfriend after Mum left. Whenever Justine brought up the subject he would say, *I've got a daughter's love—that's good enough for me.*

I've got a sister's love, even though we'll be apart. That's good enough for me.

The Urban Rest Stop—a place for homeless people to shower and brush their teeth and do their laundry for free—is my final landmark. Two men in hooded sweaters are outside the first door of the Stop—one, bearded and smoking a cigarette, leans against the bike rack; the other is sitting cross-legged next to the metal garbage bin. Both look scary, but I am calm. The police station is close. I know what to say if they ask for money: "Mo' money, mo' problems." It's not needed; neither man watches me or changes his behavior or says anything as I pass by.

Then I am at the corner of 9th and Virginia Street, standing before the Seattle Police Department—West Precinct. The rectangular building occupies the entire right block, all the way to 8th Avenue. Along the main body are concrete columns. Directly above each is a stacked trio of windows joined to an overhang by two short poles. They look like a team of Transformer guards tucked away, standing watch over Virginia Street; and when called upon in times of crisis, they will step out of their nooks, assume their true identities and stomp any bad guys on the loose. At the far end of the building, an American flag is tied to the top of a pole, fluttering in the breeze. From my study of Google Maps, I know the flag is outside the main entrance. I head for it, passing four different varieties of police car along the way. When I enter the courtyard, I sit down on one of the concrete blocks near the steps. Going inside is not part of the plan. In my head I can see the crazy-busy scene with phones ringing and keyboards clacking and investigators discussing clues to a baffling case and handcuffed criminals shouting for their one call. I think I can complete my mission here, outside the building. And to make sure I am not ignored, I decide to behave the way my disability is shown in movies and on TV. I bow my head, cup my ears with my hands, slowly rock backwards and forwards, and groan loudly.

It doesn't take long—not even three minutes. A pair of black boots appears on the strip of concrete occupying my field of vision. A female voice asks the exact question I was hoping for.

·············●···········

"DO YOU NEED SOME ASSISTANCE, SIR?"

"Yes, Miss Officer. I do."

"O-kay. What can I help you with?"

The policewoman is not very tall, maybe five feet three inches. Several white hairs—most likely from a dog—are stuck to the cuffs of her trousers. I can see the outline of a bulletproof vest under her blue shirt. Her round face doesn't have any freckles or wrinkles. There is a small mole under her chin. Her expression is even, not angry or upset, but not cheerful either. She wants to know I'm not wasting her time.

I sit up straight and focus on the tip of her nose. "I would like to get in contact with my sister, Justine. We got separated at Pike Place Market."

"Okay. Can I ask your name, sir?"

"Perry Daniel Richter. Like the scale."

"Perry Richter. Age?"

"Nineteen years old."

"Judging from the accent, I'm guessing you're new to this area."

"We are on holidays from Australia."

"I see." The officer lifts the baton from her belt and holds it up. "That's not a knife!"

The reply is both surprising and confusing. More random outbursts? First the girl on the street, now the policewoman. Is it just them, or is weird behavior normal in the USA? I think I would have to stay awhile and meet a lot more Americans to know for sure.

The officer puts the baton away and gives a small cough into her closed fist. There's redness in her cheeks. I don't want her to feel embarrassed, so I direct my vision toward the tag on her pocket. It shows her name: Pam Bassi.

"Your sister?"

"Yes."

"Does she have a cell?"

"A prison?"

"A cell *number*. A mobile phone number."

"Yes."

"And what's your sister's name again?"

"Justine."

"Okay. Well, if you'd like to come with me, we can call Justine from the barn."

Officer Bassi mounts the first step leading to the station house. I clap my hands twice and shake my head three times. She freezes the way I used to when I played Statues in elementary school.

"I want to stay here," I say. "I have a brain condition that causes me to feel anxious or upset in different places

148

and circumstances. I have trouble with people—mixing with them and communicating with them—and it sometimes results in inappropriate behaviors. I appreciate your understanding and patience."

Officer Bassi takes her foot off the step and stands facing me, legs shoulder-width apart and hands on hips. She turns her head a fraction and stares at me. Her question is obvious: *Are you pulling the wool over my eyes?* I'm set to assure her I'm not when she exhales and lifts a mobile from her pants pocket. "Good speech, Perry. What's your sister's number?"

I tell her. She enters the sequence and puts the phone to her ear. I imagine Jus on the other end, feeling the vibration against her thigh. She whips the "cell" from her shoulder bag, stabs the green button, shouts into the receiver. Her free hand clutches her head. A line of sweat is visible on her tank top. The strands of hair not caught in her ponytail can't hide the angry sunburn on her neck.

"Hello. Is this Justine Richter? Ma'am, I'm Officer Pam Bassi from the Seattle Police Department…Yes, yes, ma'am…Calm down—he is here with us…He is fine. Absolutely fine, ma'am…He was somewhat distressed when I first encountered him, rocking and making noises…Yes, he told me about his condition…"

I lift my legs up onto the concrete block and cross them over. For a split second, my mind returns to the scene around the corner: the two men outside the Urban Rest Stop. Is anyone searching the streets for them?

"…We are at the West Precinct on Virginia Street, between 8th and 9th…No, he's not. Perry requested he remain outside…Yes, he was quite firm about it…You sure you know where to go?…Okay, we'll see you soon… Yes…No problem, ma'am. Goodbye."

Officer Bassi returns the phone to her pocket and takes a seat on the concrete block beside me. "Your sister will be here shortly."

"Thank you, Officer Bassi," I say. "Now, could you leave me alone?"

"I'm sorry?"

"No lie—could you leave me alone, please?"

I know I am being rude, and Officer Bassi's features— a single arched eyebrow, tongue pushed up under her top lip—show disappointment and unhappiness. She is looking for an explanation. I have one to give her.

"I would like my sister to see me as strong. As independent. I don't want her to think I need a policewoman to stay with me and hold my hand."

Officer Bassi's face changes. Her gaze shifts toward Virginia Street, then to the sky, then to her lap. Maybe she thinks other explanations are nearby, floating in the air, lying at her feet. She stands up and adjusts her belt. "Okay, Perry Richter from Australia. This is your show.

150

You know where to go if you're not feelin' the strong man."

I nod. "Thank you. I do."

There's a small pause. Officer Bassi opens her mouth to say something; nothing comes out except a small laugh. She shakes her head, walks up the stairs. "Take care now, Perry."

When she's halfway toward the "barn", I shout out a final thank-you. She gives a small wave but doesn't look back.

..............●●●●●...........

JUSTINE STILL ISN'T HERE. It's been twenty minutes since she was called.

That's too long. It took me twenty minutes to get from Pike Place to the police station, and I was on foot. Justine is not on foot—she has the Cobalt. Perhaps she got stuck in traffic? Or there were delays because of the building construction on 9th Avenue? Even so, she should be here. It's been too long.

My body is beginning to shake. All over. I'm like a jackhammer on this concrete block. A big, shaking, anxious jackhammer. I think I made a mountain out of a mold hill. A huge mountain. I wanted to make my sister afraid so she wouldn't cancel my move to Fair Go. I tried to set her free, but I went too far.

I see what is coming.

It isn't Justine.

She's not on her way to pick me up. She doesn't want to rescue me. She can't do it anymore. At this very moment, my sister is in the Cobalt, speeding back toward the Canadian border. She will get on a plane and go back to Brisbane. She is free, but I am not responsible. She freed herself.

Fair Go doesn't exist now; I am headed somewhere different, somewhere close by. And Officer Pam Bassi will take me there. She comes out of the barn and, without a word, pulls my hands behind my back, handcuffs me. She puts two fingers in her mouth and whistles. The ground rumbles, sirens wail. The Transformer guards step out from the walls and move down Virginia Street, crushing cars and knocking over streetlights. When they move in beside Officer Pam Bassi, I see they have brought a pair of companions: the scary men in hoodies. A chill runs down my spine. My stomach turns to water. The Urban Rest Stop—the place for the homeless, the place you go when no one is searching for you anymore—that's where they're taking me. The hooded men close in. They smile, revealing teeth that are yellow and gross. The bearded one with the cigarette has a bike lock and a samurai sword.

The other whispers, "Mo' mountains, mo' problems."
I scream and try to slip out of the handcuffs. They hold
tight, biting into my wrists like a—

·····•••••••●•••••••····

"OH, PERRY. WHAT. THE. SERIOUS. FUCK."

The cuffs vanish. My panic evaporates. Justine is the
only person on Virginia Street. Her face is full of debris.
Tear tracks, like the San Andreas Fault, run from her
lower lids to her jaw.

She approaches with fast, clomping strides. Eyes
slitted. Teeth gritted. "What the hell were you thinking
wandering off like that? I had no bloody idea if you were
in trouble, or hurt, or-or-or kidnapped. Or dead!"

Storm clouds have gathered directly over her head.
Lightning bolts touch down in her hair. Steam pours
from her ears.

"Do you have any idea how freaked out I've been? For
fuck's sake, Perry, you're nineteen years old!" Standing
face-to-face, she hits my shoulder. She slaps me in the
chest. "Honest to God, for a moment in the car, I thought
about just driving away."

She stops. Her eyes grow wide. She lifts a hand to
her forehead. The lightning shorts out, the steam thins,

then disappears. The storm clouds begin to separate; there is a cautious sun peeking behind, wearing zinc cream on its nose. I look over Justine's body. It is smaller than usual, pulled in tight. Her hands are clasped together now, pressed against her chin.

"Oh, shit. I shouldn't have...I didn't mean to say...I would never actually..."

She is ready now.

Say it, Justine. Say you can't do this anymore. Be strong and brave.

She grabs handfuls of her hair and pulls.

············●···········

SHE SAYS, "YOU'LL BE GLAD to see the back of me when you move to Fair Go, won't you?"

············●···········

SHE REFUSES TO LOOK ME in the eye. I concentrate hard on her face, searching for any hint of a joke or a lie or a joking lie. There is none. I speak slowly. "So, I am still moving to Fair Go...That is still our plan, yes?"

Jus nods, grasps the middle, ring and pinkie fingers of my right hand. "Of course it is, of course." She tightens the hold on my hand, like it's a lucky charm she doesn't want to lose or have stolen. "I'm so, so sorry for what I said just now, for losing it. For losing *you*. Oh God, can you forgive me, Pez? Please say yes."

"Yes," I reply.

"You mean it?"

"Yes, Just Jeans."

She hugs me, lets her head flop back. She says a bad word to the sky, then looks forward again. "I want to cry but I won't."

........•.........

WE WALK SIDE BY SIDE to the Cobalt, parked near the public library on Virginia Street. I have questions for my sister: *You can't do this anymore, right? Why do you think I would be glad to see the back of you? How come you are so, so sorry?* I don't ask these questions though. I keep them to myself. The answers would probably get in the way of what's important. And what's important is not what should've happened, or what should've been said, or why things didn't go exactly to plan, or why people—even those closest to you—can be as confusing and random as the scene of an earthquake. It's a puzzle too hard to piece together, a mystery too big to solve. The only solid objects I can grasp right now are the only ones worth holding onto.

Justine is free.

Perry Richter, Master Disaster, saves the day.

···········●···········

ON HIGHWAY 5, PASSING through the town of Blaine, I remember an essential topic Justine needed to discuss with me on our return journey to Vancouver.

"The pen pal we are going to meet, the one who rang you in Peachland," I say. "You said you would tell me about her on the drive back from Seattle."

Justine sits up straighter in the driver's seat. The rhythm her thumb was tapping out on the steering wheel slows, then stops. She sniffs and tugs her earlobe. "I did tell you that, didn't I."

"I would like to know her name. If I know her name, she won't be as much of a stranger and then I won't be as nervous."

"Yes."

"And I didn't ask you about it every half hour these last few days, did I?"

"No, you didn't."

"Did you forget?"

"I didn't forget, Pez."

A hush settles over us. I have nothing else to say. Jus stays silent until we see the giant white columns of the Peace Arch and the lineups for the Canadian border crossing.

"I know I said I'd tell you on the drive back," she says, scrunching her eyes tight for a second, then opening them wide. "And I don't want to break my promise. I just think…it's been a long day, mate. A lot has happened—too much. That's on me. I just think you need a rest. *I* need a rest. The day doesn't need to get any longer."

"I don't understand, Justine."

She sighs. "I'll tell you all about my pen pal tomorrow, bud. After we've had a good night's sleep. The sun'll come up and it'll be a whole different day. We can start fresh."

Justine squeezes my shoulder, then resumes her previous tapping rhythm, this time on the dashboard. I nod, slowly. I count the cars in the border lineup once, twice. After the second count, I reach over and collect my seismometer from the backseat. It's the first time today I have held the small dome. It feels good, smooth and comfortable in my hands. I place it between my feet. It will remain there for the rest of our drive, until we reach our hotel. I might even keep it on the bedside table tonight.

···········•·············

THE SOUND IS COMING FROM THE iPAD.

A mix between a siren and a phone ring.

I pause Jackie Chan mid-kick in *Supercop* and make my way to Justine's hotel bedroom. I turn the doorknob very carefully and push the door open, maybe thirty centimeters, enough to fit my head through the space. Even with the outside light sneaking in, her room is dark. Dark and quiet. Except for the snoring. I can just make out Jus: lying flat on her back, her left arm bent over her head, her right arm flopped out over the side of the bed. I smile—her "sleepy monkey." Dad called it that. He said an earthquake wouldn't wake her when she was in that position. I don't think that would be true—unless it was minor, maybe between 3 and 3.9 in magnitude. I close the door and return to my room.

Opening the iPad, I recognize the sound—it's a Skype call. Justine loaded Skype on here a few weeks ago in preparation for my moving out. She has only added two contacts so far, the first being her own. Unless she's phoning me from her dream (she did say she's been having some crazy dreams), it's the second contact on the line.

Marc.

I stare at the green button that will answer the call and load the video connection. It pulses like a toxic bubble. I narrow my eyes to slits so they don't begin to hurt. Why is he calling? It's over—Just Jeans was very clear, even from the perspective of a disabled person having a meltdown. She said this was too much to handle. She said she didn't need the extra aggravation. She wanted Marc to leave her alone. She had no clue for how long. I'm confident three days is not long enough.

The siren ring is like a sharp pencil poking my eardrums. I turn the volume down but the green bubble doesn't shift, doesn't fade away. Could I just ignore it? It might ring all night. Marc might've fallen asleep at his computer, the mouse still in his hand. If that's true, the only way to stop the call is to answer and wake him up. And whether he's asleep or not—it's highly unlikely given it's close to 6 PM back home—it's good manners to acknowledge someone you know when you see them in person. Of course, I haven't seen him in person yet, but I know his face is waiting behind the green bubble.

I press the button. The circling arrow appears. Marc Paolini—the man who needed to be a boyfriend, not a hero—travels halfway around the world in three seconds and enters our hotel room.

........●........

"HEY, PERRY."

"Hello, Marc."

"I figured if I got an answer, it would be you. Thanks for picking up."

"You're welcome."

"I realize it's late there…What is it? Midnight?"

"Twelve-oh-nine."

"Is Justine awake?"

"No."

"Okay, good. I'll keep this short and to the point."

"Sure."

The resolution of the picture is a bit fuzzy, but it's still obvious Marc doesn't look so hot. There are bags under his eyes. Lots of spiky stubble on his chin and cheeks. His hair is sticking up like he's in an electrical storm. In the bottom right corner of the screen, I can see a beer bottle that looks empty. Marc could do with a visit to the Urban Rest Stop.

"You're actually the one I wanted to talk to, Perry. Well, you're the only one I *can* talk to now, thanks to my stupidity."

I don't know what to say to this, so I squeeze my hands into fists and think for a few seconds about Ogopogo in his lair under Rattlesnake Island. I'd like to collect my seismometer from the bedside table, but it is rude to just get up and walk away in the middle of a conversation. Watching it with my peripheral vision—that will have to do.

"I just wanted to apologize…to you, Perry. Justine has told me in the past how you lose it when she gets upset. No doubt it would've been real hard for you the other day. That was my fault, all my fault. I'm sorry for the pain I caused you. Very sorry. I hope, you know, we're still cool."

I examine the evidence. Yes, Marc's *ridiculous* phone call at Okanagan Lake made Just Jeans cry and caused me to have one of my worst meltdowns in a long time. But it also resulted in me seeing Ogopogo and figuring out how I could set my sister free, although it didn't work out exactly as I'd planned. In the end, just as much good as bad, maybe more.

"I think we're still cool, Marc."

"Yeah?"

"Yes."

"For real?"

"Yes."

"You're not joshin' me? I know you're like Jackie Chan—pretty good with the jokes."

"If I was joking, I would've said you weren't forgiven until you stopped wearing cologne."

He nods, gives a tiny smile that lasts a nanosecond. "Cheers, Perry. Your forgiveness is important to me." He leans in. I can almost trace the red lines on his eyeballs. "One thing before I let you go. I would appreciate it if you could keep this conversation between the two of us and not tell Justine. I'm not talking to you now because it's a sneaky way to stay in touch with your sister. I'm not ignoring what she said. I just felt I needed to make amends with you. That's all. If we could leave it at that, I think it would be best."

"Sounds logical."

"Okay, great." He runs a hand through his electric hair. "Righto, then. I don't want to keep you at this time of night. Thanks again, Perry. I won't be Skyping you again, or anything else. Not until—"

"Until Justine is finished with you leaving her alone."

"Yeah. When she's finished. When I've earned some of her forgiveness. Okay, take care, Perry."

"Take care, Marc."

"I hope your time in Vancouver is…I hope it's all good."

"We're meeting Justine's pen pal tomorrow."

"Ah, pen pal…I hope it goes well."

"Thank you, Marc."

"Goodbye, Perry."

"Goodbye, Marc."

I turn off the iPad, shut down *Supercop* and climb into bed. I look forward to the time when Jus is finished with Marc leaving her alone and he's earned some of her forgiveness. He may not come back as a soul mate or a boyfriend, maybe not even as a Skype contact.

A pen pal, though. That could work. Jus does like having a pen pal.

············●●············

18 November 2007

I was staring at a blank page for a long time before writing this. It's almost three o'clock in the morning. You and Perry are sound asleep. Neither of you seem to have been disturbed by my swearing, my pacing, my talking to myself or my crying. I'm thankful for that. My wish is that the two of you have the best sleep you've ever had, full of the greatest dreams the universe can muster. I don't think that's too much to ask, given what's in store when the sun comes up.

I've got cancer, Jus. Bad. Probably about as bad as you can get it.

I got the confirmation today. It's in the pancreas and it's advanced. I'd had this ache in my guts for a while that would also give my back hell from time to time. Thought it might've been all those years in the workshop catching up with me, or maybe an old surfing injury. I'd been losing a bit of weight, too (I remember you'd mentioned it a few times).

I went to Dr. Gerschmann a couple of months ago for an initial checkup, so she sent me on to the oncologist. He did some tests and they turned up a whole mess of tumors. Gave me the news this afternoon. I asked him if they could do anything about it. Anything at all. Before he could answer, I launched into telling him about your great-aunt Megan's breast cancer, how it had been aggressive, how they'd given her less than 50 percent chance, how she was in remission and still well and truly kicking around now. I'm a single dad and I got twin kids, I said. One who's seventeen going on thirty, one who's seventeen going on ten. There's got to be something you can do. I can't be leaving them alone. The doc said they'd do chemo, but it would only be to "improve quality of life and gain a modest survival benefit." I asked him what the hell that meant. He gave me six months and a brochure on coping with a terminal illness.

God in heaven, how am I going to tell you, Jus? And Perry. How am I going to make him properly understand? And how will he take the news? What's he going to do? Get upset? Get all confused? Will my Master Disaster just keep looking at his earthquake books like he didn't hear a word?

I remember when your mother left, you took it upon yourself to explain it to him. You were four years old. That's not happening this time.

I just looked at the clock again. It's almost six. There's a peep of light coming through the window. My head is a spinning top. My hands are cardboard cutouts. The cancer's eating away at my insides like a Tassie devil.

I hear feet moving in Perry's room.

JUSTINE

THE FIRST CONTACT—THE ICEBREAKER (OR perhaps Arctic shelf-breaker would be more accurate)—was a sixteenth-birthday card. The words are still fresh:

Wishing you and Perry every joy on your special day. If you have any interest in writing back, please send to the address on the envelope.

I really hope you do.

Your mother, Leonie

I did reply. It was a book report on my life. I described my best birthday—my thirteenth—spent riding the roller coaster at Dreamworld and surfing a Boogie Board on the waves of Burleigh. I told her I'd read *The Handmaid's Tale* in eleventh-grade English. I wrote about Perry. His typical days at school, his typical evenings at home. His success at riding a bike and his failure to understand personal space. His willingness to try fish for the first time at Rainbow Beach.

My second letter was a carbon copy of the first. News, insights, anecdotes. No queries or speculations.

No reference to the monstrous white elephant straddling a dozen years and the blue expanse of the Pacific Ocean. I imagine she was surprised (and probably relieved), but she had to know an envelope stuffed with reckoning was inevitable. I mailed it six weeks later.

I got my answers.

It's time for Perry to get his.

As we step onto the crossing, headed for the front entrance of River Rock Casino, I try to gauge my brother's state of mind. He's the same as this morning. When I told him my pen pal just happened to be our long-departed mother, his response was not what I had imagined: *Rice Bubbles are called Rice Krispies in North America. I think the Australian name makes more sense.*

He's similarly detached here on the cusp of this earth-shifting moment. The large revolving door providing entry to the casino is much more interesting—it has people-sized plant arrangements in its design. And the speed of its rotation, though not fast, has him considering the implications of a misstep. Right now, there isn't room in Perry's head for feelings on what is about to transpire. I'm sure he has them, though. I think he packed them in the backpack, along with the seismometer and Ogopogo and *Rumble in the Bronx*. They'll be taken out in due course.

Emerging from the doorway, I scan the foyer. Can Leonie pick us out of a crowd? I provided photos—the most recent from a few months ago. There are plenty of people around, young couples that could conceivably be mistaken for us. I note one pair standing at the nearby information map, studying passersby; they're definitely looking for someone. The girl looks the part: she's around five-seven, early twenties, better figure than mine. The bottle-blond bob doesn't fit with the images sent though. The guy...He looks nothing like Perry. Not that Leonie would have much of a clue anyway. None of my snaps gave her a decent idea of his appearance. He was always looking down or looking away or holding something in front of his face.

Can our mother find us?

Can we find her?

Ninety-eight...ninety-nine...one hundred. Ready or not, here we come!

We stop and I check my watch. Six minutes to ten. The bleeps and buzzes of the slot machines continue to spill out of the entrance. Bells ring, announcing a win for some lucky punter, but no shouts or whoops or cheers follow. A sign near the ATM says *Know your limit.*

The clone couple at the map continues to search the space. They turn slightly left, where carpeted corridors lead to a side entrance. A burst of recognition strikes the girl. A man wearing a turban and a business suit meets her advance, and the trio plunges into a clumsy, chattery, happy group hug. Something about the scene triggers a voice inside me, sharp and insistent: *Turn around, walk to the parking lot, drive your brother back to the hotel. Offer apologies by phone, send regrets through the mail.*

I elbow the thoughts aside and urge Perry—suspiciously eyeballing a rack of *Moose on the Loose* T-shirts at a nearby souvenir shop—toward the Guest Services desk.

And then I see her. Dressed in some sort of poncho. Headband. Sunglasses. Her face is too far away to match with my mind's images, but details aren't necessary. It's definitely her. She gathers up a couple of books from the small table in front—one spills out of her faltering grasp and crashes to the floor. She kneels down and retrieves it. When she stands back up, we're mounting the small staircase. Now she sees me, recognizes me. She lifts her sunglasses to her forehead. The look on her face says, "You got me." She raises a hand, gives an abbreviated wave. I wave back. I tug Perry's elbow, but he's brought the seismometer and seismograph out of the backpack and is gathering data. We mount the final step as an automated voice shouts, "Jackpot!" followed by the sound of coins toppling into a catch tray.

·········•·········

"HOW ABOUT A HUG."

She searches my face, peers into my eyes. "Are you sure?"

I take the backpack from Perry (he's still analyzing the data) and put it down in front of me. It's like a chock holding my feet in place, preventing me from slipping. "I think affection can be shared between pen pals."

The label is a blow to her, but only a momentary one. She leans forward and wraps her arms around my neck. I bring one hand to the small of her back, no other contact. The awkward embrace lasts a few seconds before I tap her, indicating time is up for pen-pal affection.

"I don't think Perry's keen on physical contact at this stage," I say, smoothing my top. "Fair comment, Pez?"

He stuffs the seismograph in his back pocket, places the dome on the floor, then unzips the backpack. He takes out Ogopogo and tucks it under his arm. "I don't like to touch strangers. You are my mother, but I consider you a stranger at the moment. I really don't know you well enough yet."

Leonie nods, gives a thin smile. "Of course."

The dialogue stalls for a few seconds. Leonie takes off her poncho and folds it over her arm. She's quite a yoga advertisement, our mother: arms toned, stomach flat as a board. Her posture is perfect. Given the chance to trade bodies with her, I wouldn't hesitate. From the neck up? Another story. She looks wrung out, spent. Her eyes are heavy, perhaps weighed down by the bags under her lower lids. Her top lip has a crop of deep wrinkles. The hair pinned under her headband is dull and brittle. The combination of hoary features and awesome body is unsettling. She resembles some cautionary tale from Homer or Ovid—a poor victim of the gods, cursed with an eternal contrast of youth and age.

Perry stares at his interlocked hands. Another jackpot announcement drifts across the foyer. Leonie points to the books in the crook of her left arm.

"I've got something for you," she says too quickly, too loudly. She hands them to me. "It was pretty clear from your letters that you love novels—thought you might like a Canadian classic. Mordecai Richler. And you mentioned Perry's into hurricanes in a big way."

"Earthquakes. He's interested in earthquakes."

"Oh."

I hand the copy of *Lost in Katrina* to Pez. He places Ogopogo on the floor by the seismometer and thumbs through the pages.

"I'm sorry, Perry. I can take it back if you would like a different—"

"Some American people have said Hurricane Katrina was worse than the earthquake in Haiti," he says. "It's not true. There were hundreds of thousands of people killed in Haiti, not just thousands. And the earthquake provided very little warning, whereas many people had warned the US government about the city of New Orleans flooding and they didn't listen. I think the only people who believe Katrina was worse are American. They've probably never visited Haiti or even seen the devastation on the Internet."

I can sense Leonie looking my way, seeking some sort of guidance. I keep reading the back cover of *The Apprenticeship of Duddy Kravitz*.

"Um, yes. You're probably right, Perry. Would you like me to return it?"

He closes the book, leans it against the seismometer. "Thank you, I would like to keep it. I think there will be an interesting story and a lot of interesting information in *Lost in Katrina*."

"Okay then. Awesome."

He raises a thumb in an exaggerated fashion, then points to the Washrooms sign. "Excuse me. I'll be back shortly."

He hesitates for a moment under the arch, unsure which corridor matches the sign's arrow. Then he walks on, obscured from view.

"Does he need help?" asks Leonie.

"He's fine. He gets weirded out if he has to use gross public toilets. Porta-potties—he hates them. But hey, who doesn't?" I close the novel. "He's quite capable."

She nods and watches as I stuff Ogopogo and the two books into the backpack. "He seems to be handling this situation pretty well."

"We came prepared."

"You mean the stuff in the bag?"

I zip the bag shut. "Among other things."

"So you told him about me?"

"Of course."

"How did he take it?"

"Snap, crackle and pop."

"What?"

"Better than I thought he would. He wasn't angry or scared, didn't get upset. He accepted it—the reality of it, not so much the implications. Maybe Extrasensory Perry had a little inkling of news on the way before I told him. You never want to underestimate him in that regard." I steal a peek at the arch. No sign of a return yet from the toilet. "He has questions, you know. Lots of questions."

"That's fair."

"He wanted to know what I thought."

"Did you tell him?"

I scoff. "No way. None of this is going to come from me—it's going to come from you. He deserves the same courtesy I received."

"Absolutely. He does. I didn't mean to imply that, you know, you had to or anything."

I wave dismissively and scan the foyer—the cavernous ceilings, the stately curved escalators. "This is more like a cathedral than a casino. How come you wanted to meet here?"

She shrugs. "No special reason. It's about halfway between my place and where you guys were staying in the city. And I know River Rock."

"You gamble a lot, then?"

"Sometimes. Not a lot."

"Often enough to feel comfortable here."

She shakes her head. "I'm not really built for comfort."

Perry appears in the walkway, rubbing his hands on his thighs. As he moves in beside us, it's clear he's agitated.

"Troubles in the bathroom?" I ask.

He nods.

"Let me guess…hand dryer?"

He nods again. "It was very loud. Like a leaf blower. I don't think I've heard one like that before, in Australia or North America."

I pick up the seismometer from the floor. "Need this to help out?"

He shakes his head. "I think I'll have the book instead."

"The Newcastle earthquake one."

"No, the brand-new book. The present from her. *Lost in Katrina.*"

Leonie throws me a glance of…I'm not sure what. I think she's a bit stunned. Intrigued too. And is there a small sense of satisfaction? If there is, it better be smaller than the odds of a win in this casino.

"Okay, then." I extract the hardback, hand it over. He opens to a random page and holds it close to his face. "How's that?"

He bounces the book up and down. "It smells very good," he says, voice muffled by the fan of pages.

"We're going to leave now. Are you right to head back to the car?"

"Yes."

As we move in silence toward the parking lot, bells and whistles split the air. Another jackpot has landed. It's only an impression, but it seems there's a lot of good fortune in the building this morning.

........•••••••••.......

FOLLOWING LEONIE DOWN THE 99, an earlier statement drowns the song on the radio. *He seems to be handling this situation pretty well.*

Perry's handled squat. He's still engrossed with everything but the situation. On the way out of the casino, he pointed out the Canada Line and went to town on a 2009 tragedy at Walt Disney World in which two monorails collided and a twenty-one-year-old driver was killed. Passing under the digital signs displaying US border information, he wrote down the various wait times and delays. And, at this moment, he's thoroughly impressed with Mount Baker, standing imperious and white-capped on the southeastern skyline.

"You know it's a dormant volcano, don't you, Just Jeans?"

"I do now."

"And you know about neighboring Mount St. Helens and how it exploded in 1980, distributing a drift of ash that reached Australia?"

"That I did know."

Extrasensory Perry. He has questions, you know. Lots of questions.

He will make his inquiries when he's ready. And our mother will answer each one. My hope is that her answers will be worthy of his understanding and forgiveness. It's not as unlikely as it seemed a week ago. He accepted *Lost in Katrina*, even chose it as a source of consolation after the toilet panic. Thus far, although distracted, he's at least been calm.

Good ol' Mount Baker.

Lots of questions.

Of course, there is always Mount St. Helens. If it happens, if explosion results...Well, second time around, our mother must do better. She must stand still, even as the ash spreads far and wide.

That's the answer I'm looking for.

·············●●●···········

"SO, WHAT HAPPENED AFTER THE boat ride on Okanagan Lake?" asks Leonie.

I wince. Not the question to ask, Leonie. Not at all. I look left into the living room, then at the half-empty bottle of champagne on the table. My mind ticks over, revisiting the drama, choosing words. I shift to Perry. *The Tuxedo* is on *pause*. He's slid out of the armchair and onto his knees, hands over his ears, his breathing heavy. His gaze is fixed on our mother. It's like he's prompting memories, cueing her recall. Remember this?

Remember the last time you saw me unravel? I'm older now, but it's still the same when things go wrong. It's hard. On me. On everyone.

Leonie is an abandoned ventriloquist's doll—limp, slumped, mouth open. Understandably, she can't figure how it all soured in a matter of seconds. Perry was settling in so nicely. Upon arrival, he checked out his room, put clothes in the wardrobe and drawers, found homes on the shelves for all his security items. He ate lunch at the outdoor setting in the courtyard. He listened in on plans for the stay: Whistler tomorrow, PNE the next day. When she let him know the PNE was Vancouver's equivalent of the Ekka, he clapped his hands and nodded approvingly. And he didn't bat an eye when informed it would just be mother and son for the show; I would head downtown for some R and R. For the last half hour, he'd been content to play with his iPad and watch Jackie Chan. Now he's on the verge of coming apart, courtesy of a ten-word question she thought was more innocuous than a falling snowflake.

I gulp some bubbly, clear my throat. Perry, still peering over the edge of reason, has shifted attention to me.

"It's okay, mate," I say. "I'm not going to lose it again. I'm just going to tell her what happened."

"No lie?"

"No lie. I'm just going to tell the story."

"Ogopogo isn't around to help me if you cry."

"You won't need him, Pez. Promise."

Perry lifts his hands from his head and drops them by his side. He stays perched on his knees.

"Marc and I are on a break," I say. I down the remainder of my drink, then refill my glass.

"Is there more to the story?" asks Leonie.

I tell her about our agreement, how I needed temporary distance so this trip could be the sole focus. Then I sketchily detail the calls—at the Pacifica West, on the Coquihalla, the third, backbreaking breach by the lake. I don't reveal how Marc's views on this little family reunion paved the way to the parting.

"He apologized for ringing the first two times. Howzat, hey? He *rang* to say sorry for ringing."

Leonie draws a smoke from the nearby packet, taps the filter on the table. "Yes, that's bad."

"It's complete overkill."

"Yes."

I lean forward, elbows propped on the table. "You don't sound convinced."

"No?"

"No. You think I'm making too much of it."

"I never said that."

"You don't have to. It's in your tone."

"I'm going outside." Leonie jumps to her feet. The force of the movement rocks the chair. It teeters for an instant on two legs, threatening to topple, then crashes back down into the backs of her thighs. She rides out the clutch of pain, steps away from the table and fumbles with a lighter on the sideboard.

"I'm coming with you."

"You don't smoke."

I move in front of Perry, bend down and cup his face in my hands. "You seeing me, Pez?"

"Yes."

"You okay if we go outside for a bit?"

Perry checks the wall clock. "It's eight fifty-one. Why are you going outside?"

"Mother-daughter chat."

We step through the sliding glass door and into the back courtyard. Standing side by side, we observe the glubbing fountain in the center of the cheap water feature. I know the setup to our story is done. It's time for the conflict and, one way or another, the resolution.

"I'm sorry," she begins. "You've made a decision and I support it."

I scoff. "Smile and nod, hey? You don't get off that easy."

"I'm trying to do the right thing here."

"Then do it. Communicate. Don't cave." I pick up a withered maple leaf lying on a nearby stone, twist the stem between thumb and forefinger. "We're grown-ups, Leonie."

She lights the cigarette, takes a long calming drag, blows smoke out the side of her mouth. "Look, obviously I don't know Marc from Adam. The little I do know I got from your letters, and from what you wrote he seems like a pretty nice guy. You certainly liked him when you put pen to paper—I don't think there's any doubt about that. You wrote about possibly taking the relationship to the next level—moving in together at some point in the future, after Perry was settled. Clearly, the two of you had plans."

I drop the leaf, watch it float down and come to rest by my feet. "There is potential."

"And, look, I know things have changed because of the calls. You see him a bit differently now—God knows, I can relate to that. Story of my life in a lot of ways. But here's the kicker, Justine: he cares. He doesn't make those calls if he doesn't care. I'm wondering how much you've really thought about that."

"There's a big difference between caring and need-lessly interfering."

"Maybe he just needed his hand held. Never needing your hand held, or at least refusing to admit it...I think that's a hell of a lot worse than needing it a bit too much."

I fold my arms, nudge a loosened rock back into place with my toe. "You're talking about Dad now, aren't you?"

Leonie flicks the spent cigarette onto the pathway and crushes it underfoot. There are a few butts discarded on the ground.

"You knew Dan as a father," she begins. "He was a great father. From day one, he was smitten with the two of you. He played with you, bathed you. Read to you at night. When he'd come home from work late—he hated the times when he had to work late, just *hated* them—all he'd want to do was talk about his 'twinnows.' He'd want to know every last detail: what you'd eaten, how much you'd napped, what sort of poop you'd produced in your diaper. When he went out, he'd always take you two with him, even when you were tiny; he'd lug you around in one of those baby carriers like you were his passport to the world. He took you to the beach, to the playground. Hell, he even came up with an exercise routine using those damn carriers. I was only around for four years, Justine, but I saw enough to know what he was. He was meant to be a dad. He was *born* to be a dad." She glances at me, ekes out a thin smile. "You don't need me to tell you that—you knew how good he was."

I look skyward, then at the back of my left hand. "He was the best."

She nods. "And as good a father as he was, he was a lousy husband, Justine. I never wrote about it in any of the letters I sent to you—there wasn't any point.

But I think there is a point now, so I'm going to tell you. He had no time for me. All the things he gave to you two—the love, the care, the concern—he tucked it all into bed with his twinnows at the end of every day. He was a lousy husband, Justine. I can say it in 2010. I was able to say it after the divorce, too, when the blinders came off and I saw things more clearly. In the midst of the marriage, though, I was struck dumb. We shared what I thought was love, but then it began to fall apart, week after week, month after month, until it was nothing but an obituary. Actually, not even an obituary: just an obscure moment in history or a boring trivia question."

I shift my weight, pick some lint off my sleeve, shift again.

"I tried to salvage it. I cooked his favorite meals: veal parmigiana, shepherd's pie, snapper with slipper lobsters. I always, *always* asked him questions about his work before I launched into my day. I bought lingerie even though I couldn't stand to look at my post-baby body in the mirror. None of it made a blip on the radar. When I left, I let him have it. It was his fault. He was a shitty husband, he was a heartless bastard. He'd held a life jacket in his hand while he watched me drown. I gave him hell, but deep down, I didn't believe any of it—I was the shitty one; I was at fault. I'd failed my marriage. Add to that my abject failure as a mother and it was clear what must be done:

I had to go away, take my failure elsewhere. Dan would find another woman, a better woman, one he could love as much as his twinnows." She crosses her arms, rubs the rising goose bumps. "Turned out I was wrong, eh? Dan might've been a born father, but he was born to do it alone."

The sun is almost gone and lights are on in the neighboring townhouses. There's a chill in the air. It might be the result of the nearby flowing water, or maybe the Canadian summer is ending already. I look over at my mother. She's shivering, seemingly at the mercy of the cool change. I'm not feeling it. In fact, my armpits and spine and hands share a tickle of perspiration.

"So, Marc deserves a second chance and Dad didn't," I say. "Is that the gist of what you're arguing?"

"I'm not arguing, Justine. You told me not to cave, you said communicate—that's what I'm doing. I'm not arguing. I'm just saying, that's all."

"And what exactly are you saying?"

"I'm saying the same thing I said at the start: Marc cares. He's phoning you up because he cares. And there are worse things in the world than that."

Yes, there are worse things. You would know, Mum, wouldn't you?

I hold my tongue and examine the palm of my left hand. When the last cheap jab has cleared from my thoughts, I respond, "This trip is about Perry, not me.

You need to ask his forgiveness. You need to win him over. And you need his permission if you're really going to become part of our lives again. I think you should focus on that, Leonie." I move toward the sliding door, stop, backtrack. "No offense, but you're not the one to give me advice about relationships."

When I reenter the living room, Perry is sitting in one of the armchairs, wearing a blanket like a bonnet.

"I didn't listen," he says. "It's wrong to eavesdrop."

"Thanks, Pez."

"That's why I'm wearing this over my head."

"Wearing what?"

He pats the blanket, pauses, then laughs. "You got me!"

I smile and suppress a pretend yawn. "It's been a big day. More adventures tomorrow. Time to hit the hay, I reckon."

Inside my room, I look out the window at the courtyard below. Leonie is still there. She reaches down, scoops water from the stream and splashes it onto the back of her neck. Then she walks back into the house.

·········●··········

MY NIGHT'S REST IS INTERRUPTED around a quarter to five. After a few seconds getting my bearings, I hear muffled conversation from downstairs. I tie up my hair, put on trackpants and socks, then poke my head out of the bedroom. The light is on in Perry's room—no signs of life though. I pad past and ease onto the stairs. At the third step, I kneel down and peer through the gap in the handrail. Leonie is doing yoga. She's chatting with an unlikely spectator.

"Is everything okay, Perry? Do you need something?"

"It's difficult for me to sleep."

"Oh. Is your bed uncomfortable?"

"No, my bed is okay, thank you. I'm having trouble sleeping because there is a lot of change happening. Things are different."

My brother is standing at the far wall, observing with his peripheral vision. He picks up a small crystal object—a Buddha, if I'm not mistaken—from the shelf by his elbow, replaces it, then moves in beside the armrest of the couch. "Do you feel different?"

"Yes, for sure. Maybe not as much as you. But, yes, definitely I feel different."

He gives three of his big over-the-top nods. "The readings certainly indicate things are different."

"Readings?"

He points toward the upstairs rooms. "From my seismometer. The ground is shifting, I reckon."

The surrealism of this scene is not lost on me. It's just after five in the morning, eighteen hours or so behind

Brisbane time; I am huddling on the steps of a town-house on the outskirts of Vancouver, Canada, spying on a chat between my runaway mother and extrasensory brother. Leonie Orr, whom I know from photographs and fan mail, who took off while we were dreaming four-year-old dreams, who threw us in the too-hard basket. Our mother: no longer running away, now settled, still, present. Our mother, the grown-up.

We're all grown-ups, Leonie.

"Would you like a drink, Perry? Or something to eat?"

"No, thank you."

"Would you like something to help you sleep?"

"Like milk?"

"Sure. I have other stuff, too. Stronger stuff than milk."

"Medication?"

"Yes."

"No, I don't take medication. Only Tylenol if I have a headache. Dad said I never needed medication. Just Jeans agrees." He bends down and runs a hand over the smooth rubber surface of the yoga mat. "I think I'll stay up, if that's okay."

"Of course." Leonie glances at the staircase. I shrink back. "Do you...do you want to talk?"

"About what?"

"Well, I understand there are things you want to ask me."

Perry stands to full height. He directs his gaze to the bookshelf in the corner of the living room. He makes a pair of fists, as if he's trying to squeeze the questions from the palms of his hands. My heart is jumping. My mind is a whirl. Of the thousand and one answers my brother deserves, which will be the first?

"Can you show me how to do some of your exercises, please?"

Leonie is as surprised as I am. She leans to the right, attempting to catch Perry's eye. "Are you telling another good joke?"

"No."

"You really want to learn some yoga poses?"

"Yes."

His eye is still elusive, but there's no doubting the conviction in his voice. Leonie retrieves a second mat from behind the armchair and lays it out next to hers. Perry positions himself beside her and reties the cord on his pyjama pants.

"Before we start, can I ask why?"

"Why what?"

"Why you want to learn some yoga poses."

Perry blinks several times. "I am taking an interest in what you like to do. That is good social skills and helps build good relationships. It's what grown-ups do. Do you agree?"

She nods in reply. "Yes, it's what grown-ups do."

·············●●············

LEONIE TEACHES PERRY A SERIES of stretches called Sun Salutation. Before performing the exercises, she gives him some background to the routine—its origins in praise of the Hindu sun god and how it is part of a Hindu person's daily chores. In response, he shares the scientific skinny on the sun—its chemical composition, consisting largely of helium and hydrogen; the temperature, coming in at a balmy six thousand degrees Celsius; and the life cycle, counting down to the ultimate demise in around five billion years.

"It will change from a yellow dwarf—what it is now—to a red giant, and its diameter will probably reach Earth. If anyone is still here, they'll be burned to ashes."

Leonie informs him there will be Canadians tanning right up to the end, and he commends the attempt at comedy with a spontaneous round of applause. Then they begin the movements—mother demonstrating and son copying. Perry's enthusiastic and eager to learn the original terms, repeating them after he's performed a pose.

I'm surprised by Pez's efforts—he's no stringbean. For a guy of strapping build, he shows a pretty decent level of flexibility. A prayerlike stance progresses into raised arms, forward bend and all fours. When they arrive at a prone position—a pose Leonie calls the Cobra—Perry doesn't arch his back or lift his chin. He stays flat on the mat, head sideways, right ear to the floor, like an Indian scout from an old-time Western. Leonie asks him if he'd like some help, then suggests physical assistance: bringing her hands up under his armpits and lifting him into the pose.

"Are you okay with me touching you?" she asks.

Pez grunts—it sounds like "Go ahead." Leonie kneels beside him, hands at the ready. She's hesitating. I lean into the rail, thrumming with suspense. Physical contact is a big ask for Perry, but it's clearly no picnic for Mum either. I can see memory is weighing upon her. That or something else. Guilt, maybe. She reaches forward, tremors in her hands. The rest of her body is tense, reluctant. Her arms slide through the spaces between Perry's burly shoulders and the mat; his armpits settle in the crooks of her elbows.

"Is that okay?" she asks, voice cracking at the final vowel.

There are no cryptic grunts this time. His response is clear. "Yes, Leonie."

Her name. It's the first time he has used it, first time he has viewed her with something other than curiosity. I hold the rail so I don't fall down the stairs.

"Would you like me to help lift you into position?"

"Yes. If you would like to."

She heaves her arms back. Perry levers his chest off the mat and curves his spine in yoga-textbook fashion. "You should try to look up at the ceiling rather than sideways."

He smiles. "Are you afraid of being bitten by the Aussie cobra?"

By the third run-through, Perry knows the routine and is posing independently. They perform side by side in silence, bodies stretching and flexing in unison. I watch several more poses, resisting the urge to demand more conversation—ideally, on a topic more substantial than yoga terminology—then steal back upstairs. Inside my room, the sun is streaming through the window, awakening to the first day of the rest of its five-billion-year life.

·········●··········

DESPITE THE INTERRUPTED SLEEP, I'm fresh and alert guiding the Cobalt along the Sea to Sky Highway south of Squamish. Leonie, in the passenger seat, holds an unlit cigarette in her fingers. Perry's crashed in the back, head drooped forward, snagged seat belt preventing any butting of the headrest.

"You guys were up early," I say. "You have a chat?"

Leonie half-smiles. "We did talk. Mainly about the sun."

"Really?"

"Perry wanted me to teach him some yoga, so I showed him *Surya Namaskara*. He repaid the favor by telling me about how the sun is a superlarge ball of awesomely hot gas. Then we did the routine for a good half hour or so."

"Wow, that's great!"

"He told me he was taking an interest in what I do. He said it's good social skills, helps build good relationships."

"Sounds like him," I say, adjusting my sunglasses. "He's certainly making an effort."

We stop in Squamish and eat at a restaurant called Naked Lunch. Perry and I share a number of jokes and one-liners: the customers are drop-ins from a nudist colony, a chef in his birthday suit should be careful with hot plates and sharp knives, "tips" for the service staff could take on a whole new meaning. The laughs between us come thick and fast.

"You two are so good together," says Leonie. "So in tune with each other."

"We are twins," I reply.

"Are we?" adds Perry, holding his stomach and wiping a tear from his eye.

"You sure are," continues Leonie. "You are *Namasté*, the palms of two hands in perfect symmetry." She runs her straw down her glass, drawing a line in the condensation. "It makes me a bit sad to think the two of you will separate when you return home."

Like a glass knocked off the table, my good humor plummets, shattering into pieces. I ask a passing waitress for our bill. Pez says nothing—it appears Leonie's lament went right over his head. He's still got the giggles.

"Tell me more about this Fair Go place," says Leonie. "Are there plenty of activities?"

I press an index finger onto her lunch plate, lifting away the leftover crumbs of panini. "Activities? Jesus, it's not a Contiki tour, Leonie."

"I know. I just meant...I meant—"

"Services?"

"Yes, services."

"They've got prevocational opportunities and paid 'job' work. That happens during the week. They offer all sorts of stuff: woodworking, arts and crafts, landscaping, IT, care for animals. They have stuff specific to the campus too: kitchen work, cleaning, recycling, basic handyman maintenance."

She turns to Perry. "Are you interested in any of those?"

"Not really." He's noticed the change in my demeanor. Consequently, he's serious now too. "It's good to try different things."

"That's true. But it would be nice if there were some choices you liked already."

"I s'pose. Maybe they will have yoga."

"He knows he might not get to do the same things as before," I say.

"The woman director said they could provide some car-wash responsibilities for me," adds Perry in a loud, authoritative voice. "And first aid. I might be able to assist in teaching some of the other residents."

Prompted by Perry's volume, an elderly couple, seated at the adjoining table and festooned in cycling spandex, glares our way. I engage them with a smile.

"My brother has a brain condition that causes him to feel anxious or upset in different places and circumstances. He has trouble with people—mixing with them and communicating with them—and it sometimes results in inappropriate behaviors. I appreciate your understanding and patience." I join my hands together in front of my chest. "And if you don't have any understanding and patience, Mister and Missus Tour de Pants, then hop back on your bikes and bugger off."

They turn away, hunker down over their BLTs and mutter a few choice words about the "Australians ruining Whistler." Leonie mouths the word *wow*. I counter her praise with a shrug.

"It's important to be ready for stuff that happens in public. People treat disabled adults a lot different than kids."

The theme of preparedness continues on the way up the mountain. Perry crashes again, and I take the opportunity to speak candidly. I plunge into the PNE trip tomorrow and the laundry list of challenges my mother will have to deal with. Places, people, sights, sounds. "Be aware of how he's coping," I say. "Look for signs that things are starting to go sideways. We saw them briefly at the casino, and again last night during the Okanagan recount: nervous flicking, fast breathing, putting his fingers in his ears, rubbing his hands up and down his thighs, a gradual lowering of himself toward the ground. If any or all of these are happening, it is crucial to distract, redirect. Get in his face. Tell him to look at you, to focus on you. Ask him if he's seeing you. If that does nothing— if the words are going in one ear and out the other—then use one of his comfort items to snap him out of it. Put it in his hand. Drop it at his feet. Hold it against his skin. And please, try to use an item that's right for the moment. If there are creeps hanging around, stay away from some of the less age-appropriate items. He doesn't need any extra embarrassment.

"Stay close," I add. "He's having to cope with a lot. I really underestimated that in Seattle."

She nods and vows to remember all I've said. And I don't doubt her promise. But remembering is a lot easier than doing. Doing is hard.

Like staying.

··········•●•··········

IN WHISTLER, WE SIT FOR a time on a patio nestled at the foot of the ski hill. All across the slope, mountain bikers leap and fly and spin on a steep, dusty course of jumps and ledges, both man-made and natural. Perry watches the action like a kid on Christmas Day—wide-eyed, unblinking, mouth open, barely comprehending the sensory-overloaded scene. After ten minutes or so, he studies the drop closest to us, his face a mask of solemnity.

"Problem?" I ask.

He stands, ignoring the query, and approaches the patio rail to gain a closer look at the drop. He returns half a minute later, frowning and shaking his head. "There is instability here too," he says. He turns to Leonie.

"Remember this morning? I said there was a lot of change happening?"

"Yes."

"You remember my readings?"

"Yes. You said the ground is shifting."

Perry nods. "I thought we might get away from it today, but it's here too."

He bends down, rubs his hands together, places them on the ground. He takes the seismometer and seismograph out of his backpack. The dome is placed on the deck under one of the adjoining tables; the reader finds a home under Extrasensory Perry's nose. After a brief scan of the results, he mutters a word I can't recognize, packs the equipment away and inhales.

"What was that you said, bud?" I ask.

"*Pranayama*," Leonie says, stubbing out her cigarette. "It's a yoga term for controlled breathing."

I must have missed that one. I begin to speak but am interrupted by a proclamation.

"There will be a crash soon," Perry says, balling his hands. "The earth is loosening up."

I lean forward, elbows planted on the table. "Have you noticed a problem with that jump over there, Pez? Is it unsafe?"

The question is ignored; the frowns and fists continue. "*Pranayama*," he repeats.

Leonie and I study the jump in question. The first half dozen mountain bikers negotiate the launch and landing without a bobble. The seventh—a bug-eyed dervish with curly red hair spilling out of his helmet and tattoos snaking down his arms—doesn't fare as well. His takeoff is different from the previous riders: he attacks the far left lip of the ledge. In midair, he twists the front wheel left, then right, then back to center, positioning it ideally for a balanced landing and quick getaway toward the finish. The ground, though, fails to reward his skill. As the tires strike, the solid terrain disintegrates. A chunk of the track spits out sideways from the front wheel. He holds the jackknife for an instant, then he's a projectile, careening over the handlebars, vainly clutching at thin air. When body and hard pan collide, Perry's mantra pierces the air.

"*PRANAYAMA!*"

And then we are on our feet. Astonishingly, so too is the fallen rider. Amid the swirling dust, hunched and hurting, he scuttles over to his bike and inspects the damage. The front fork is bent. The handlebars are pushed back. The chain has come away.

"Are you okay?" says Perry. "I can help you."

Tattoo Guy throws a glance Perry's way but doesn't respond. With his one good arm—the other is pressed to his chest, clearly injured—he stands the bike up.

"I have a first-aid certificate."

He loops the chain back over the cog. Within sixty seconds, the spectacle ends. Tattoo Guy wheels his bike through a flagged marshalling area and disappears into the crowd.

"His face showed embarrassment and anger and fear," says Perry, resuming his seat. "And I'm pretty sure he's dislocated his shoulder. That would require a cuff-and-collar sling rather than a regular sling for a broken arm."

"You knew," Leonie says, breathless.

"What?"

"You knew he was going to crash."

Perry frowns and shakes his head. "I didn't know *he* would have an accident. I don't know him at all."

"You knew something was going to happen, though, didn't you?"

"Yes. It was obvious."

Leonie turns to me. Her gaze is hopeful, pleading for some shared sense of awe.

"The patch of ground was like two tectonic plates," Perry continues. "When the bike landed, it came down on the fissure, which is the gap between the two plates. The lower one pressed into the higher one and caused it to fly out of the ground. It was like a tiny version of a 9.0 tremor."

Leonie wants another cigarette, but the pack in her purse is empty. She keeps searching, pulling out several empty pill bottles. Perry's declaration from this morning surfaces in my thoughts: *I never needed medication.*

"So, this is what you meant?" she asks.

"Pardon me?"

"Before, when you talked about the shifting ground?"

"There is instability here, like I said."

She bites her pinkie fingernail, nods. "You said it's at home, too."

"Yes."

"Is something going to happen at home, Perry?"

He sniffs and flicks his hand. "I don't know what you mean."

"Something like we just saw? Something unexpected?"

"I don't know."

"You don't know?"

He flicks his hand a second time. "It's not obvious like today was."

"Do you suspect someone might get hurt?"

"No."

"No one will get hurt?"

"No, I mean *I don't know.*" Perry takes hold of his right earlobe in a pincer grip. "I would prefer not to talk about this."

"It's okay. I'm just trying to understand."

"Yes, but I would *really* prefer not to talk about this!"

"Leave it there, Leonie," I say. I take hold of Perry's wrist and give three quick squeezes. "That's enough 'trying to understand' for now."

She can't let it go though. Approaching Horseshoe Bay on the return journey, with my brother fast asleep for the third time today, she draws me back into the paranoid analysis. "What do you think is going on in his head?"

"When he's napping, you mean?"

"No, with the whole shifting-ground-instability-at-home thing."

I prop my elbow on the open driver-side window and rest my chin on my hand. "You want to know what I think? I think he's got an inkling of what we're about to ask him, of the say he has in our future. In *your* future."

Leonie glances over her shoulder. Perry is snoring. "You think he knows I want to come back?"

"I reckon he might."

"And the fact that he will decide if it happens…You think he sees that?"

"No, I don't think he"—I use air quotes—"*sees* it. He's just making some logical conclusions, putting two and two together. He's quite capable."

"I think he's more than that. I think he's gifted."

"No, he's *capable*. He's more aware than most of the world around him. He notices things in people that might not be clear to others. He takes in a lot—more than he's equipped to handle, in fact. He senses energy and he feels change. Does that make him worthy of respect? Absolutely. Does that make him...I don't know, the Oracle of Delphi? Hardly."

"He has a gift, Justine—I'm sure of it. The third-eye chakra. The *Ajna*."

"No, he doesn't."

"He really is Extrasensory Perry."

"Not the way you see it." I take my right hand off the steering wheel and pat my forehead with the heel of my palm. A short, abrasive laugh leaps from my throat. "Boy, after all these years, you still want to think of him as a freak of nature. A handicapped freak as a child, a gifted freak as a man. He's not a circus act, Leonie. He's just different. Okay? Unique. He's loving and caring... The best brother I could've ever had. And he shouldn't be tagged with a label, certainly not one from a bloody chakra chart. Okay? He's just like the rest of us—amazing in his own right, and no better or worse than anyone else."

The argument slides into silence. On the winding Sea to Sky Highway, we pass cars and cars pass us. Near the turnoff for a place called Cypress Bowl, Leonie opens her purse again and rummages around. A spare cigarette in the clutter? A pill that escaped from the bottle and is lying among the shopping receipts and spare tampons?

No. She takes out a cloth to wipe the smudges from her sunglasses.

Are you seeing me? That's the question she should be answering.

And Perry should be the one asking.

·········●·········

"PEZ, CAN WE HAVE A CHAT?"

Perry closes *Lost in Katrina*, stands the book on the adjacent shelf and joins us at the dining table. He looks to Leonie, then to me, his face impish despite the stubble on his chin and cheeks.

"This is like the interrogation scene in *Police Story 2*," he says, smirking and feigning cuffs on his hands. "That is an okay joke."

I nod. "Yep, could've been better. Listen, we want to talk to you about something."

"Is it to do with Leonie coming back?"

My heart vaults to the top of my rib cage. I throw a stern look Mum's way—a warning to keep any *Ajna* chakra gibberish to herself. She clears her throat and drains the dregs of her third rye and ginger. "It is, actually," I say, maintaining a watchful eye. "You had a suspicion of it, didn't you?"

He unlocks his invisible cuffs with an invisible key. "We are going back to Brisbane in two days—I thought Leonie might be coming too."

"Leonie would like to come and live in Australia again, yes."

"Is she coming back to be a proper mother for us?"

I glance at Leonie. She's like a human house of cards, afraid of collapsing with the next breath of air, staring at her clasped hands on the table. One thumbnail is wedged under the other, digging, probing. I'm on the verge of suggesting the question can be answered another day when she decides the time for a response is now.

"I imagine I would be...someone you could get to know, Perry. Over time. I think that would be the way to start out."

Perry considers this for a good ten seconds, then nods. "Is she..." He stops, clicks his fingers, shakes his head. "It is bad manners to speak like this when the person is in the room and can speak for themselves." He eyeballs the vase of carnations by Leonie's left elbow. "Are you catching the same flight as us?"

"No, she's going to—" I press my fingertips to my lips, extend a hand toward our mother.

"I wouldn't come back straightaway," she says. "I would settle things here, make some calls to people over there. Could take a little while. A few months at best."

"I will be at Fair Go by then. It would be you and Just Jeans living together."

"Um, it wouldn't be…That could be—"

"Pez, Leonie wouldn't move into our house," I say. "And right now, Leonie returning to Australia—it's actually not a done deal yet. It needs to be something both of us agree is okay."

"Both of us?"

"You and me."

Through squinted eyes, he looks at Leonie for the first time in the conversation. "Just Jeans and I will decide if you move back to Brisbane?"

"Yes."

"Just us. Not you?"

"I went away. It's up to you if I can return."

"You are an Australian citizen—you could return whether we wanted you to or not."

"I wouldn't do that."

"You could though."

"I wouldn't do it. I want to come back and be with you guys more than anything I've ever known, anything I ever will know. But I won't come back unless the two of you allow it."

Perry wipes the back of his hand across his mouth and starts making little grunting noises in his throat. "Have you decided?" he asks me.

"I'm not going to say at this point."

"I think your face says you've decided yes. Is that correct?"

"Pez—"

"I would support your decision if you've decided yes."

"Perry, you can read my face, my hands, my eyes, my toes…I'm not going to tell you what I'm thinking about Leonie's return. Okay? This is something you must decide without knowing my opinion."

Perry rubs his eyes with his balled fists. I move in beside him and put an arm over his shoulders. Our mother rises from the table and makes to step away.

"Stay there."

She resumes her seat.

"You've got a full day together tomorrow, Pez. Just the two of you at the PNE. See how it goes. See how you feel at the end of it. Then we can talk about what happens next."

He nods, gives me a hug, then collects *Lost in Katrina* from the shelf. He flicks through from start to finish four times in quick succession, the pages blurring like hummingbird wings.

··········•••••••··········

3 April 2008

I'm sorry if this is hard to read. The numbness in my fingers is making it tough to write without it looking like a mess of chicken scratches. It won't stop me doing your journal though. I promised I'd do it right up to your and Perry's eighteenth birthdays, and nothing—not cancer or chemo or numbness or nausea or fevers or kidneys being on the fritz or losing weight like a jockey or bloody World War Three starting up—is gonna get in the way. Not with a mere six months to go until the big one-eight.

I'm not much into religion, Jus, but I've been trying to convince God that He should throw a miracle our way. Mainly at night, I've been chatting with Him. I hope you don't mind—I've been using you as the big guns in my argument. I said it was pretty poor form for Him to give you such a dud hand. A teenager having to defer uni to care for her terminal old man and her disabled brother... How can He justify that? And then there's the fact that you do everything—and I mean EVERYTHING—without a sigh or a sullen look or a single complaint. Without a split second's thought for yourself. Why would He treat you so badly? Why would He punish one of His most beautiful angels?

I haven't even mentioned how your mother skipped town. Might add that one to the plea bargaining tonight. You asked awhile back if I should get in contact with your mother to let her know what's going on. My answer is still the same: What's the point? She hasn't dropped a line or sent a postcard or even requested to become a bloody Facebook friend in the fourteen years since she took off. Why would she want to be in contact now? Because I'm dying? She probably thinks I had it coming. No, I see no need to reach out to someone who walked away without the slightest peek over her shoulder. Unless, of course, she's been belted with the generosity bat and would like to donate her pancreas, spleen, liver, lungs, etc., to a good and worthy cause.

PERRY

I CAN SEE IT.

Screaming and flailing. Punching my head, kicking the wall. I don't mean to be violent. I don't want to be out of control. It just happens. And I'm hardly aware it is happening. That's because my mind has gotten smaller, lost a few of its other functions. It's gone into fight-or-flight mode, as if I'm a caveman confronted by an earthquake or a dinosaur attack. Actually, some scientists call it the reptilian brain response. But I'm too young to know any of that. I'm only four years old.

I'm in the middle of the floor now, standing on my toes. There are blood-smeared tissues lying all around. And one in Mum's hand. She's holding it up to her eyebrow. I can see she has two purple bruises on her arms. She has a big purple-yellow one on her calf too. They look like they were drawn on with markers; I sometimes do that on my own skin. And the walls. And the clothes in the laundry basket.

She leaps forward and wraps her arms around me. I scream and throw my head back. We twist and stumble, headed for the floor. Then my arm is free, out of her hold.

I swing and hit Mum on the side of the face. My eyes dim. Static fills my ears. Slowly, the reptilian brain begins to crawl away. I feel the floor under my hip and shoulder. And I feel Mum's body behind me. And her arms across my chest. I stare at the fingertips of my right hand before reaching back to touch her cheek. It has a long scratch on it. If I knew anything about quakes and plates and fissures, I might imagine it as a fault line. I don't.

I'm only four years old.

············●●●············

WE PASS THROUGH THE TURNSTILES at ten o'clock. I look around and right away I feel less anxious. Just as Leonie said, the PNE is very similar to the Ekka in Brisbane. The rides, the food, the crowd. The dirty people who are in charge of the attractions—the people Just Jeans calls Carnie Schwarzeneggers. One thing about the PNE is different though: the old Wooden Roller Coaster. It is the reason I have excitement as well as anxiety. As we pass by a group of pale teenagers talking about the Zipper, I decide to share some of my recent research findings with Leonie.

"The Coaster was built in 1958 and is made of Douglas fir. It has a top speed of nearly eighty kilometers per hour.

It was in two movies—neither of them was very good and Jackie Chan wasn't in them. I don't think there have been any major accidents, not like the Timber Wolf ride in Kansas City, America, where a small girl was thrown out of the cars and died."

"Would you like to go for a ride?"

"Yes, I certainly would."

I have three turns on the Coaster, one straight after another. Each time, I have to wait patiently in line and listen to the Carnie Schwarzenegger's instructions about keeping my arms inside the car. But then during the ride—particularly the big drops—everyone lifts their arms up and screams. So I do it too, so I don't come across as a weirdo. And when I come back to the Carnie Schwarzenegger, I apologize for not following his instructions. He chews his gum and repeats the same things he told me before.

"How did you like that, eh?" asks Leonie when I return.

"I didn't get thrown out."

"That's good. You looked great up there. Just one of the gang."

"No one else was saying *pranayama* when it was over."

Following the Coaster, I have rides on the Enterprise, the Pirate Ship and the Hellavator. When we arrive at the Westcoast Wheel, I ask Leonie if she would like to join me. At first she says no, but when I'm almost at the front of the line she changes her mind. Two minutes later, we are suspended high above the PNE, the two of us together in a cage, defying gravity, looking out over a city that doesn't know it is being watched.

·············●············

"ARE YOU AFRAID OF EARTHQUAKES, LEONIE?"

"A little. Probably no more than the average person living in this city, I would say."

"No lie, seismologists believe there's a 37 percent chance of an 8.2-plus event and a 10 to 15 percent chance of a 9.0-plus event in the Pacific Northwest sometime in the next fifty years."

"And what does Extrasensory Perry believe?"

I shrug. "I can never be sure whether something will happen or not. Nobody can, not even the best seismologists. I know one thing definitely, though: if it happens, living in a world of one is not an option. People will need each other."

On the ground, I notice a man in a wheelchair on the path below the West Coast Wheel. An overweight woman pushes the chair with one hand; the other hand shoves a melting ice-cream cone into her mouth. When they reach the end of the path, the woman loses her grip.

The chair hits a metal garbage bin, and the man gets thrown forward like a crash-test dummy. He groans and a long line of drool hangs out of his mouth.

"Whoops!" says the woman, pulling the chair free and keeping the ice cream away from the spazzing man. I watch until they disappear into the crowd.

"Is a fear of earthquakes one of the reasons you'd like to come back to Brisbane?" I ask.

"No, that hasn't really entered into my thinking."

"Brisbane is a good choice. Brisbane doesn't have fault lines like here."

"I've got one reason for coming back, Perry. Well, two, in fact."

"I think it would be difficult living on a fault line."

"Lots of people choose to," Leonie replies. "They accept it."

"Some don't. Some move away."

The wheel shifts for the third time on our ride. It is our turn to go to the very top. There is a large bird— maybe a hawk or a bald eagle—flying in the distance, making figure eights above the houses. It looks similar to the one Ogopogo was watching at the lake. I wait for the cage to stop rocking before I speak again.

"Where did you go after leaving our family?"

Leonie sits up straighter and uncrosses her feet. She grabs hold of the nearest bar in our cage. "I, uh…I lived with my mother—your grandmother—and my step-father in Cairns. She wasn't too happy with me being there and you guys being back in Brisbane. We argued a lot. I moved out after about nine months."

"Is my grandmother still alive?"

"No, she died toward the end of 1995."

"Just Jeans and I were maybe five. Did we ever meet her?"

Leonie closes her eyes for an instant. She swallows, and it sounds like there is glue in her mouth. "Yes, a few times. When you were little."

"I don't remember her."

"She loved you two. She didn't spend as much time with you as she should've. I'm to blame for that."

I move my head from side to side. Then I take the seismometer from my pack and place it on the seat. The Westcoast Wheel's clunky motor kicks in again. Our cage starts steadily arcing back down to earth.

"Do you need to smoke a cigarette, Leonie?"

"I'm okay."

"I don't like cigarette smoke. It chokes my throat and my skin. And it dries out my eyes. But we are outside, so it won't affect me much."

"I'm okay."

"Are you sure?"

"I'm sure."

"So, you're not addicted to smoking?"

"No, I'm not addicted, Perry. I've quit lots of times."

I nod as we reach the ground and come to a stop. "You don't have to quit again because of me."

········•••••●•••••••·······

WE ARE SEATED ON A bench near the bumper cars, eating lunch. I've got chicken strips and chips. Leonie has a burger. She throws it in the bin after two bites.

"When did you leave Australia?" I ask.

"After my mother died."

"Where did you go?"

"I backpacked around Europe, South America, parts of Asia. I ended up in India, living in an ashram."

"What is that?"

"It's a quiet place away from the world, where you can study and pray and meditate."

"And do yoga?"

"Yes. I learned yoga and how to teach it in the ashram."

I tap the seismometer with my fingernail. The *plink, plink* sound it makes—it resembles dripping water.

"And then you went to Canada?"

"Yes," she says. "I came here after India. My biological father was Canadian. I'd never met him, so I thought it was about time I did."

"Did you live with him too?"

"No. It took me a long time—almost a year—to find him. He worked in the Alberta oil fields and on the ice-fishing boats that go to Alaska. I managed to meet up with him in a town called Red Deer. It was brief, awkward. He barely remembered Mum. At the end, he shook my hand, thanked me for tracking him down. He said he would try to keep in touch, but I knew it was a lie. I haven't heard from him since." She shrugs. "He wasn't cut out to be a parent. That sounds familiar, doesn't it?"

I don't know how to answer that, so I scrunch my face and make some popping sounds. Then, after thirty seconds, I rock back and forth. Leonie asks if I'm okay. My eyes spring open and the next question pours out of my mouth like lava from the vent of a volcano. "How long after meeting your biological father did you write to Just Jeans?"

"Two weeks."

I nod three times. Leonie gets a look on her face that I can't properly read.

"Did you see that before I told you?" she asks.

"See?"

"Did you know that fact before I told you?"

"I knew you probably would've written soon after. It's a logical conclusion." I shift the seismometer to my lap. "Did you ever think about writing a letter before that time?"

Leonie leans forward, elbows on her knees. Her hair blocks her face. It looks like a small gray-streaked curtain has been lowered down over her eyes. "I thought about writing or phoning or getting in touch years before I did, but I never got beyond thinking about it. I couldn't find the words. Every sentence seemed like an insult or an excuse or a sick joke. The more time passed, the more I felt like there was no way back. And that was fitting. You guys were better off without me." She touches the front of her throat. Perhaps she has some burger stuck there. "When I met my dad, I realized I was different from him—I cared. I was a disgrace and unworthy of forgiveness, but I cared. So I bought a birthday card, wrote in it and put it in the post before I had a chance to lose my nerve."

I push my fists into my ears and jump to my feet. I lift the seismometer from the bench and place it under my nose. "Can you hold this for me, please?"

She brings a hand up to her forehead to shield the sun.

"I would like to go on the Crazy Beach Party ride. My brain is getting packed too tight—no lie, it needs to loosen up. Can you hold my seismometer for me, please?"

After a four-second delay, she stands.

"No, no! I need to go by myself." I move the seismometer to the crook of my left elbow and pat her shoulder with my free hand. "Please sit down."

She obeys and takes the seismometer.

"One ride will be enough. I'll be back before you can say, 'Ogopogo was here.' Promise."

Then I go on the Crazy Beach Party ride.

Twice.

Just to make sure.

·············●·············

"WHEN YOU LEFT OUR FAMILY, did you leave because of me?"

I ask the question three seconds after sitting down on the bench again. Leonie almost drops the seismometer as she's handing it back to me. "I didn't leave because of you. I left because of me."

"I have an excellent imagination, but my memory is very good too. I was a problem child. A big problem child. Breaking toys and screaming and hitting and kicking. I hurt you."

"No. You didn't."

I look her over. "Your right foot is bouncing and your earlobes have turned red. You are not sure."

"Yes. I am sure."

I frown and twist my lips, but I don't want to say she is not telling the truth. "Dad never said I was a 'problem'— he used to say I was a 'handful.' What would you say I was?"

"I'd say you were…challenging."

"Challenging? That's similar to 'problem.' And more accurate than 'handful.' I think I was two hands at least, maybe a foot as well. I was a problem child. A big problem child."

"I left because of me," she repeats. "I felt it was all too much, and getting away was the only real solution. I thought it would make everyone's life easier if I wasn't around. That might've been true for your dad—we didn't get along very well. But you and Justine—me becoming a ghost, letting you down, not being there for you as you grew up—that was a mistake. A terrible mistake."

Leonie slides off the bench and onto her knees, facing me. "Can I take your hands?"

I hesitate, then offer them up. Her fingers are thin and rough. The skin on her index finger has a yellow-colored stain. She's trembling.

"I'm sorry. I'm so, so sorry. I know I can't possibly make up for the past. But this could be the start of a new future, if you want it to be."

I roll my shoulders and begin to hum. I don't want to look in her eyes, so I stick to staring at our intertwined fingers. "It's all too much and getting away is the only real solution," I say. "That's how I feel quite often. I think we have that in common."

"You think so?"

"Yes, I do. In fact, if things had been reversed back then—if I were the mother and you were the child—I think I would've made the same mistake. So, really, you're not the only one." I take my hands away and cup her face. "Are you focused?"

"Yes, I am focused."

"Are you seeing me?"

"Yes, I am seeing you."

"Good." I nod three times. "You should come back to Australia."

"Do you mean that?"

"I do. No lie."

She makes a sound, sort of a cough mixed with a sigh. "Perry, I don't know what to say. Thank you, son. Thank you for being…better than me."

"You're welcome, Mum." I lean toward her. "You are crying. Are you glad or sad?"

"Glad," she replies.

················●·············

I WANT TO BUY A SNACK and see the sand-sculpture exhibit before leaving the PNE. We stop at a stall on the sidewalk. The man behind the counter has some sort of shiny stone in one of his front teeth. I scan the chalkboard menu, then choose a bag of mini-donuts. Mum hands over the money.

"Are you getting anything for yourself?"

"I'm good." She smiles. "I am *Ananda Balasana*. The Happy Baby."

I get a picture in my head of my mother wearing a diaper and sucking her thumb. I snicker and bite into a donut.

"Do you go straight to the Fair Go residence when you get back to Australia?" she asks.

"Not immediately. I think I will head there in four to six weeks."

"That's too soon."

"How do you mean?"

"We talked about it last night—you'll be gone by the time I catch a plane over."

I shake my head. "I won't be gone—I'm just changing where I live. I will still be in Brisbane, not on the other side of the world."

"True."

"Are you afraid I won't want to see you?"

"No. It's just...I'd love to think we might live under the same roof sometime. But that's not taking you into consideration. You have every right to be independent."

"So does Justine."

She looks at me, waiting. Maybe she thinks I am joking. "Justine?"

"Yes. She has a right to be independent too."

"But she's been going it alone since Dan…since your father passed."

I wipe away the sugar stuck to my fingers. "No, she's been my caregiver all that time. That's not right. Things will be better when I move into Fair Go."

"You mean better for your sister?"

"Of course. Justine won't have to save the day anymore. She will live a normal life." I take a mouthful of a new donut. "Things didn't happen exactly the way I thought they would in Seattle, but that's okay. Justine is free now."

Mum pauses and I keep chewing. The bearded Carnie Schwarzenegger in charge of the nearby dart throw shouts at us. *Come and see if your aim is true! Burst a balloon—everyone walks away with a prize!* I tell him no thanks, I don't need a prize. We keep walking.

"You planned what happened in Seattle? The whole runaway thing—you did that on purpose so that Justine would definitely want you to move out?"

"Correct."

"And she would be free of *you*?"

I clap my hands. "You figured it out! You should be called ESL—Extrasensory Leonie! That's a pretty funny joke, by the way, because ESL stands for English as a Second Language."

"And she has no clue about any of this?"

"Of course not."

"No clue about how you feel?"

"Well, Just Jeans knows I love her."

The conversation seems to have made Mum move quicker. It's like she walked onto one of those moving walkways at the airport and I'm still on the carpet, falling behind. She gets six or seven paces in front, but still she doesn't slow down.

Hey, Mum! Wait for me!

I attempt to shout the words. Nothing comes out. I have only air in my throat. I try to get my feet moving quicker, but they are not listening. In fact, they are not moving at all. They are stuck.

And there is a weight on my head and neck and shoulders, pressing down on me as the earth rises up.

···········●···········

THE WHITE PAPER BAG IS on the street, tipped over on its side. Spilled donuts lie in the gutter. My backpack sits on the pavement, leaning left, the main compartment open and gaping. Farther away, the PNE rides are starting to have problems. The Hellavator is listing to one side. The arms of the Sizzler are wobbling. The hiss of the Crazy Beach Party has turned into a metallic roar.

Worried shouting fills my head, but it's not coming from people taking the rides or watching from the ground. Not yet.

Two pairs of women's shoes appear in front of me. Behind one of them is a set of small wheels belonging to a stroller.

"Are you okay?"

I'm on all fours. Mum had a yoga pose like this: *Adho Mukha Svanasana*, Downward-Facing Dog. This is not relaxation though. This is the complete opposite.

"Do you need some help?"

I rock forward and back, moaning. I can feel my cap hanging off my right ear. Grit is lodged under my finger-nails. The street is like hot coals under my hands. There is only pavement in front now—the women and the stroller are gone.

It's all too much
And getting away
Is the only real solution

I manage to look around for an instant. She is sitting on a bench, off to the side. Her head is down, and her lips are moving. Her hands are crossed in her lap. I think they're shaking. *Don't be frightened, Mum. Yes, the Pirate Ship is doing full circles and the Vomitron has actually turned to vomit and the wind from the Hurricane is knocking down trees and throwing benches into the air.*

But there aren't any blood-smeared tissues here. No bruises. Be brave and strong, Mum. Leap forward and wrap your arms around me. I promise I won't scream or throw my head. I promise I won't hurt you the way I did before. I'm not four years old anymore.

A pair of white Asics and blue Vancouver 2010 socks are in my sight line now. I moan and rock.

"Anyone belong to this guy?"

Murmurs, mutters. Then a clear voice. "He was here with a group of other retards."

"No, he wasn't. He's here on his own."

An arm gets placed across my shoulders. The world splits in two. I lurch forward onto my elbows, press my forehead to the pavement and squeal. I collapse onto my stomach. The hot street muffles my cries and fries my skin. One by one, the cages of the Zipper get crushed by a giant fist.

The Asics have been replaced by a pair of pale feet in sandals. A hand prods my elbow with a plastic cup filled with water.

Are you focused?

"Maybe it's heat stroke."

Are you seeing me?

"Bah! It's a damn sight hotter at the Red River Exhibition in Winnipeg and there are no folks going belly down in the street there."

You should come back.

The old Coaster—the only ride left standing—begins to shudder. The shaking builds and builds until the wooden structure can't stand the pressure. Posts split in half. Boards fly through the air. The tracks collapse, one by one. Crashing and smashing onto the ground. Sending great puffs of dust high into the sky. And when all the tracks have fallen, when it seems like no other destruction can happen, the wreckage of the Coaster explodes. The *whump* lifts the earth under my chest. The fireball consumes all the debris and the rubble and the screams of the frightened people. Then it's closing in on me, melting my skin and torching my bones until there's nothing left but—

......•••••●•••••••...

"EXCUSE ME! EXCUSE ME!"

"Who are you?"

"I am his…caregiver."

"His what?"

"He has a brain condition. It causes him to get upset in different places and circumstances. He, um, he has trouble with people—mixing with them and communicating with them—and it sometimes results in—God, how did she say it?—inappropriate behaviors."

"Where the hell *were* you?"

"I was away. But I'm here now. I'm here."

·············●●●●············

I CAN SPEAK AGAIN. PHRASES. They're tectonic plates, shifting across each other, making the needle on the graph dance.

"Too much pressure, too much buildup. Something has to give…"

"Perry, it's Mum. Can you hear me?"

"We're shaking…breaking…"

"Are you hurt, Perry? Can you get up?"

"We weren't prepared for this. We weren't ready for this."

I feel the seismometer being placed against my left wrist.

"We weren't ready…"

I feel *Lost in Katrina* nudge my right shoulder.

"Weren't ready…"

My voice trails away; only shallow breaths are left behind. Mum kneels down beside me. "Do you mind if I touch you?"

The muscle tension begins to ease. Clenched fists open. Fingers spread. I feel her arms slide through the spaces between my shoulders and the pavement, my armpits settling in the crooks of her elbows.

"Is that okay?"

I turn my head so the left side of my face is exposed. I keep my eyes closed. "Yes."

"Would you like me to help lift you into position?"

"Yes."

Her arms heave back. My chest is levered off the hot street. My spine curves. Cobra pose is held while the PNE continues, the people walking past, the rides twisting and wheeling, the sun inching closer to the horizon.

·········•●•·········

JUSTINE STANDS IN THE CENTER of the living room rug, holding her face. She yells, stamps her feet. She glares at Mum again as she drinks more of her alcohol.

"Oh my god! I. Cannot. Believe it!"

"Justine, please—"

"I thought things would be different!"

"It's not what you think."

"But I'm an idiot, aren't I? Marc tried to convince me to stay away from here. He said you couldn't change, you'd let us down. And I defended you! I defended *you* and pushed *him* away!"

"You're not looking at this clearly. The only reason I told you what happened was because I wanted to be up front, totally honest. I could've kept everything to myself and you wouldn't have been any wiser. I didn't do that. I didn't hide from the truth. And it all worked out okay. C'mon, Just Jeans."

She advances toward Mum, index finger pointing. "You do not call me that! Okay? You have not earned the *right* to call me that!"

"I'm sorry! I'm sorry, Justine!"

Jus is mad for several more seconds, then drops her hand. She hurries to the bathroom. The sound of running water is followed by splashing and the whip of a towel. She comes out again and collects the half-glass of wine on the sideboard and gulps it down. She starts pacing on the rug like one of the impatient customers at Troy's Car Care.

I can't look directly at the fighting. Staring at the pictures and the tiny statues on the mantel keeps it in my peripheral vision. I would like to go upstairs, maybe finish the last half hour of *Drunken Master II*, but I don't have enough energy to get out of the armchair. What happened at the PNE has taken my core away, leaving only the crust. I am like one of those chalk outlines of a body they draw on the ground.

Mum pours another drink. "At first, I couldn't think," she says. "I could hardly breathe."

"So, it was all about you then, was it?"

"I couldn't help Perry the way I was. I needed some distance to pull myself together."

Justine's face pinches. "Don't give me that crap. *You walked away from him. You left him.* He was face down in the middle of a street, surrounded by friggin' voyeurs, unable to fend for himself. And what did you do? The same as you've always done—*you abandoned him.*"

"It wasn't the same."

"Of course it was."

"No, it wasn't the same."

"Okay. Tell me then. How was it different? Because it was five minutes instead of fifteen years? Because it was ten meters instead of ten thousand? Because it was a grown man instead of a child?"

Mum puts her drink down on the table and enters the living room. She moves in front of a bowed Just Jeans and hunches low, trying to make eye contact.

"I came back," she says. "That's the difference. I came back."

Justine nods once, looks up. I'm only using peripheral vision, but I can tell her eyes are red. Her face is like a stone mask.

"I don't think you're going any further."

"What do you mean?"

My sister ignores the question and heads upstairs.

"What do you mean, Justine?"

Mum moves into the corridor and holds the banister for support. I can hear the sounds of packing—suitcase *thumps*, coathanger *clinks*, drawer *slams*—from the bedroom.

"ANSWER ME!"

Two minutes later, Justine drags our suitcases and my backpack down the stairs. I hear her dump them at the door, then pick up the phone. She talks to someone about an overnight reservation. She says thank you and makes another call. It's for a taxi. When she hangs up, she addresses me. "We're not staying here tonight, Pez. Okay? We're staying in a nice hotel before we fly back to Brisbane tomorrow."

I lift my chalk-outlined body out of the chair and shuffle through the living room. In the kitchen, Mum grabs Justine's elbow, forcing her to stop. "You're abandoning him, too," she says. "This moving out to the Fair Go— you're letting him walk away."

Justine scoffs. "You're pathetic." She jerks, trying to wrench her arm away. Mum holds on.

"You're the reason he's going, Justine."

"*I'm* the reason?"

"He wants you to have a proper life, and he believes he's standing in your way. When he's gone, you'll be happy. You'll be free."

"Jesus, Leonie, is this the booze talking? Where are you coming up with this rubbish?"

Mum glances at me. I move toward the door, head down, hands behind my back. I wish I wasn't a chalk outline right now. I wish Ogopogo would appear at the back door to give me a solution to this problem. I don't really want to leave. I want us to stay with Mum tonight, to use conflict-resolution skills, to do *Surya Namaskara* together in the living room before bed. I want to confirm to Just Jeans that Mum isn't lying or talking with her booze. I'm moving to Fair Go because I love my sister more than anything and I want her to be free and it's the right thing to do. But it's too late. The instability I felt, the quake I feared…it's under way.

"It's a logical conclusion," says Mum.

"Ha! Logic—your strong suit!"

"Your brother's not interested in his own independence, Justine. *He wants yours.*"

Through the blind, a green car eases to a stop outside the door. The taxi. Its *pip-pip* horn bounces off the townhouses opposite.

"If you want a pen pal from here on out," Justine says, pulling her elbow away, "write to Perry. He's quite capable." She pauses, thinks about something else, shakes her head one last time. She moves in beside me, murmurs in my ear. "Let's go."

I open the front door and drag the luggage outside. The shaking and breaking can't be stopped right now. Even if Ogopogo did appear at the back door, he couldn't help, because the only solution to this problem is to wait. We have to find a safe place until it's done and the earth has gone quiet again. Then we can look through the rubble to see what was damaged and what survived unscathed. And rebuild. It might take a long time, but you always rebuild.

Just Jeans tells the turban-wearing cab driver, "Hilton by the airport."

Before the front door closes, I hear Mum cry out, "Ask your brother, Justine! Please! Ask him before he's gone!"

And then we're gone.

•••••••••••••••••••

OUR SILENT ARRIVAL AT THE hotel is followed by a silent elevator ride up to the room and a silent sharing of room-service fish and chips. Eventually, Justine asks if I want to watch a DVD. I tell her, "No, thank you." Instead I tune the TV to the History Channel. There is a show on about the War of 1812. I watch the story about Billy "The Scout" Green, who fought the Americans at the age of eighteen and was given twenty dollars for his service at the age of eighty-two. It helps me forget for a little while about what happened at Mum's house. While I'm watching TV, Jus opens *Robinson Crusoe*, and then the book Mum gave her. She sighs and shifts in her chair, flicking through the pages rather than properly looking at them. I suspect she is thinking rather than reading. Then, around eleven o'clock, I know for sure.

"You think I overreacted?"

I turn the sound of muskets shooting and cannons firing down to zero.

"Was I being unfair to her, Pez?"

I turn toward my sister. "I think we should've stayed, used conflict-resolution skills and done *Surya Namaskara* together in the living room."

"She failed at the PNE. She walked away from you. You can forgive her for that?"

"Of course. It wasn't for long. And sometimes walking away is necessary."

"Necessary." As she repeats my word, Just Jeans pulls a face I don't understand, something combining a frown and a squint. She massages her wrist where she used to have her rubber band, then sits down beside me at the table. "Was she telling the truth about Fair Go? Are you walking away because you feel it is necessary for me?"

"I want to say no."

"But you can't, can you?"

"No."

"It's not in your nature to lie, is it?"

"I have a disability. A brain condition."

"The brain condition has nothing to do with it. You're just too good a person." She pulls me close, hugs me for nearly one minute. "Why the hell didn't you say something when Mum mentioned it?"

I flick my hands and watch a loose thread hanging off Jus's sleeve sway in the air-conditioned breeze. "Because we weren't prepared. We weren't ready."

Justine swears, closes her eyes and lets her head fall forward. She rests a hand over mine. "God, Perry, I never wanted you to go."

"I know that."

"I only agreed because I thought you wanted more independence."

"I know that."

"I am always free with you next to me, with us sharing our lives."

"I know that now."

She sucks in a deep breath, blows the air out hard. She looks up at the ceiling. "Dad, you arranged this business with Fair Go. Whatever your reasons, I know you were taking care of us. But you're gone now. We're on our own."

She drops her head and looks at me. I narrow my eyes, but only a little.

"I am focused. Just Jeans, I am seeing you."

"And I am seeing us. Together."

She hugs me again, stands and moves to the desk in the corner of the room. "So, what happens next?"

"We rebuild."

Jus nods slowly, then with increased size and strength. Three big nods. She writes on the Hilton Hotel notepad, tears the page out and folds it in two. She hands the paper to me, then enters the bathroom. When I hear the shower water running, I open the paper and read the small to-do list she has made.

Hug Perry (done)
Check status of flight
Call Mum and apologize
Call Marc and apologize
Cancel Fair Go
Rebuild

The list is very good, although the call to Mum must happen before checking the status of the flight. I get the feeling we need to contact her as soon as possible.

There is no *Cry in the shower* on the list. It should be there because I can hear Jus's small, sad yelping noises over the sound of the stream. And I feel the seismic wave building in my feet and my stomach and the backs of my eyes. But the feelings are not as painful as they usually are. They're still intense, but they're wider, more spread out. Spread out beyond my body and into the hotel room. The small table trembles. The coffeepot jumps and dances and breaks into three pieces. The bedside lamp topples onto the floor. The TV moves in and out of the cabinet on its swinging tray. And there is a shout, then a crash in the shower. Not a crash of metal or plastic. A human crash. A body. A heavy bag of bone and muscle and organ.

Just Jeans isn't crying now. She isn't making a sound.

..............●●●..............

THERE IS A LOT OF NOISE, so much commotion. Jackie Chan isn't afraid of the earthquake. He is afraid, though, when he finds Just Jeans unconscious, her whole body on the floor except for one foot caught on the edge of the tub. He is scared out of his mind.

"Jus, can you hear me? JUS, CAN YOU HEAR ME?"

Jackie Chan positions her to the side, tilts her head back. He checks for breathing by bringing his cheek close to her mouth. He doesn't feel anything. He turns her back over, checks for a pulse. No pulse. For maybe ten seconds Jackie Chan has bad thoughts: *I'm disabled, I'm a retard.*

How can I help my dying sister? He wants to lie with her on the white tiles, let the ground open up and take them both. But he shakes the bad thoughts out of his head and starts compressions. Push fast and hard on the chest—that's what you do these days. It doesn't matter so much about the thirty-to-two cycles. Fast and hard compressions are more important. And go to a depth of around five centimeters for adults. Jackie Chan knows he's gone deeper because a couple of ribs made a cracking sound.

After maybe ninety seconds, a weak pulse pushes against his fingertips. Jackie Chan repeats four times to make sure. He double-checks the breathing. It is there. He shouts again. "CAN YOU HEAR ME, JUST JEANS?"

Still no response. He has to get her to the hospital. Her vital signs are present, but they might not stay. And there might be other problems. Serious problems. Organ damage, internal bleeding. He might've punctured her lungs during the CPR. He wants to call an ambulance, but he knows the earthquake will have them all on duty. If the line isn't dead, it will be busy. He has to get her to the hospital on his own.

Jackie Chan grabs his backpack, puts it over his shoulders, tightens the straps until they bite his skin. Then he puts a towel over her naked body and picks her up in his arms. Trying to support her head as much as he can, he carries her outside. There is damage in the hallway—pictures on the floor, potted plants knocked over. Overhead lights fizz and flicker; one near the fallen vending machine explodes in a shower of sparks. He suspects the elevators won't be working, so he heads for the stairs. On the way down, he speaks to her. "It's okay, Just Jeans. I'm here. I'm prepared. I'm ready."

On the final flight of stairs, he stumbles and almost loses his grip. But he holds on. He is strong. Brave and strong. In the lobby, there are shocked people standing around, talking about what happened.

"Almost shook me out of bed."

"Got under the table quicker than a squirrel up a tree."

"Earth moved like that when Crosby scored."

Even though he doesn't like to do it, he shouts as loud as he can. "MY SISTER IS BADLY HURT! SHE NEEDS TO GO TO THE HOSPITAL!"

If there is one thing Jackie Chan has learned, it is this: nobody should live in a world of one. We need the people around us. And when earthquakes occur, people need each other even more. He knows somebody will step forward. Somebody does. A man with a long goatee beard and a Harley-Davidson T-shirt. His name is Joe. He says he heard on the radio that Richmond General is damaged and has lost power. He will drive them to Delta Hospital "super-quick."

No lie, Joe maneuvers his Dodge Challenger like a stunt car, weaving in and out of traffic, avoiding fallen trees and power lines, eluding the rubble shaken loose from shops and buildings. Through every gear change, his hands are steady, his reflexes are sharp, his face is a mask of cool control. He really should be wearing a Ferrari racing suit rather than his Harley-Davidson tee. Rounding the corner adjacent to a Chinese shopping center, they discover a Mercedes Smart car has run the red light opposite and hit a fire hydrant on the sidewalk. Water is shooting into the air, and a small lake is blocking their direct path. In a flash, Joe grabs the emergency brake and pulls, urging the Challenger into a controlled, arcing slide around the spill. He corrects the oversteer—centimeters from the far-side curb—and boots them onto the new street.

Barely a minute later, they're confronted by two stalled semis side by side on the blacktop, the space between them insufficient for a Dodge Challenger to squeeze through. As worrisome as the trucks are, of more immediate concern is the small army of sword-wielding Manchurian gangsters climbing out of the trailers and running full speed toward them.

"Friends of yours?" asks Joe.

Jackie Chan does three big shakes of his head.

"Could get a little rough here," says Joe, putting on his sunglasses.

The Challenger plows forward. Gangsters bounce off the car, shrieking like angry lorikeets, swords wrenched from their fists to *clank* on the asphalt. A few roll up onto the windshield, over the roof and off the back spoiler. One manages to hang onto the hood for a brief second before he is zapped by a stray power line and loses his grip. Twenty meters from the semis, Joe angles the right side of the Challenger at a construction ramp set up for roadworks. When the tires meet the incline, he yanks the steering wheel left and stands the car up on two wheels. Jackie Chan wishes Justine was awake and recovered and healthy so he could share this astonishing show with her—he makes do with holding her upside-down body as tightly as possible and buffering her head from the passenger door with his arm. The Challenger enters the sliver between the trucks, the spaces on either side slightly greater than the width of Jackie Chan's backpack. They hold their breath. A twitch in Joe's sure hands will see them end up hopelessly wedged and overrun by angry, concussed gangsters. The man at the controls, though, is a statue. The Challenger pierces the front cabs, emerges into open road and bounces back down onto all fours.

"This could be a movie," says Jackie Chan.

"It is," replies Joe. "Hopefully, it has a happy ending."

The biggest obstacles should be behind them, but a crisis of epic proportions still stands in their way.

Approaching the intersection that passes under the SkyTrain, Jackie Chan studies the large pillars supporting the track. Maybe it is just his imagination, but one looks slightly bowed, like it's tired and having trouble staying awake. If an aftershock hits now, the pylon could collapse, bringing the section down.

"You see it, Joe?"

"What?"

"That pillar is weak. Can we get around it?"

"Not if we want to get to the hospital stat."

Jackie Chan doesn't respond because it's too late— they're past the point of no return and the structure is indeed failing, a second rumble not required to send it careering to earth. He leans forward, trying to shield as much of Justine's body as he can. He shouts, "LOOK OUT!" as cracks in the pillar become fissures, then chunks of falling concrete. Amid the booming noise, he hears Joe yell, "HOLD TIGHT!" and feels the push back into the seat as the accelerator touches the floor.

Cars bang and crash. A motorcyclist slides across the traffic island. A van in the lane beside them wears a hailstorm of debris, then bounds up over the curb and onto the sidewalk, scattering the panicked crowds. Entering the crumbling structure's target zone, a bouncing slab clips the back right side of the Challenger, and the car fishtails. Joe pulls the steering wheel left to keep the surging vehicle on the road. Tires scream, mingling with the terrified voices of people running for cover. The deadly chaos is on top of them now. The disintegrating track is in free fall. Jackie Chan waits for the lethal blow that will spell the end, not just for Justine but for all of them. He thinks of LAPD motorcycle officer Clarence Wayne Dean, who fell to his death driving off a damaged freeway in the aftermath of the 1994 Northridge quake. He shuts his eyes as Joe blasts the horn and plunges the Dodge into the blinding fog of smoke and dust.

It's a tragedy things have to end like this.

Unlike in the movies, Jackie Chan won't save the day.

........•●•........

THE SCREEN DOESN'T FADE TO BLACK.

The credits don't roll.

He opens his eyes as the Challenger bursts from the clouded ruins. They're through! Alive! In one piece! Is it a dream? He kisses Justine on the forehead. Her right eyelid flutters in response. Jackie Chan can scarcely fathom that they're okay, out of the madness and speeding along the shoulder of the road, headed for Highway 99. They stream by gridlocked traffic on the left. They whip past telephone poles, staggered but still standing, on the right.

"That, ladies and gents, was pure balls of insanity," says Joe.

Jackie Chan looks over his shoulder and out the back windshield at the destruction. Sirens and flashing lights are everywhere. Fires have broken out in three of the surrounding buildings. Above the smoldering haze is a giant hole in the SkyTrain track.

"Givin' 'er this way, we got about three minutes to the tunnel an' about five to Emergency."

Jackie Chan tells Just Jeans to hang on. He checks her pulse (he will do so every thirty seconds from this point forward). His heart pounds and his hands are wet with perspiration. Her pulse is still there. Weaker than before, like a tiny insect trapped under her skin, but it's there. He tells her she is doing great.

"She okay?" asks Joe.

"Yes," answers Jackie Chan, trying to keep his throat open and his voice steady.

Joe swerves the Challenger around a ditched fruit truck, then holds his phone through the front seats. "You need to call anyone? Let 'em know what's happening and where you're goin'?"

Jackie Chan tells Joe he has Justine's phone in the backpack. He retrieves it and dials a number he learned by heart in recent days. The call goes to voice mail. He leaves a message of explanation:

"Mum, it's your son, Perry. Justine's hurt. She fell during the earthquake. Her heart stopped. You must come to the hospital…Don't stay away."

He has an overwhelming and terrible feeling the call won't be returned.

···········●···········

THEY SCREECH TO A HALT outside Emergency. Joe asks Jackie Chan if he can help carry Justine in.

"No, thank you," he says. "I've got it from here."

Joe pats him on the shoulder, calls him a hero and assures him the movie will have a happy ending. Joe drives away like a regular motorist and not a stunt driver.

Inside, the waiting area is busy but not crazy. There's no evidence of earthquake damage to the room itself, but there's enough among the waiting patients. A young man wearing a tracksuit and a thick gold chain holds a towel streaked with blood against his forehead. A woman with blue hair and a tattoo sleeve—probably his girlfriend— sits in the next seat, studying her black fingernails. An old couple is together near the hand-sanitizer dispenser, discussing "the rumble" and prodding the IV protruding from the man's skinny, wrinkled arm. A family of four appears to have a variety of injuries, mainly glass cuts.

Jackie Chan thinks about rocking and groaning and using other things from his disability to get some attention, but he gets noticed right away. He tells the nurse at the desk, "MY SISTER IS BADLY HURT! SHE NEEDS MEDICAL ATTENTION!"

She hustles him straight through to a room. A different nurse is waiting—she asks for "the honey-bunch" to be put down on the bed. He hesitates. He studies the nurse's face. Her brow is smooth. Her head tilts slightly to the left. There are wrinkles in the corners of her eyes. She probably smiles and laughs a lot. She looks kind. Jackie Chan lays his sister on the bed. The kind nurse tells him to wait in the corridor while the doctor performs some immediate tests. He doesn't move. The kind nurse nods and begins to examine Just Jeans. He goes out.

In the corridor, he takes off the backpack. The muscles in his arms and shoulders and back are sore. He hadn't noticed the pain before now. He keeps his comfort items close: seismometer in his lap, Ogopogo nestled in beside his right thigh, *Lost in Katrina* balanced on his chest. Jackie Chan doesn't want to think about whether Justine will make it, or the unanswered call to Mum, or the ending of this movie, or if rebuilding is really truly possible when a disaster destroys everything you hold dear. He tries to focus on other things, good things—swimming, eating chicken nuggets, surfing the Net, *Thunderbolt* and *Rumble in the Bronx*. He thinks of old memories—a wash-and-detail of a vintage black GTO he once did at Troy's, holidays at Rainbow Beach, his final day in high school. He thinks about his father's best jokes. All these thoughts help him keep a lid on his boiling anxiety.

None of them can pull out the knife that is stuck in his heart.

········•●•········

17 September 2008

Perry stayed with me while you were out shopping. He came in just after I'd woken up and sat down beside my bed. For a long time he didn't speak—he patted my hand. That's all he did. He must've stayed there for a good half hour, just patting my hand. It was a big shock, not because of what he was doing, but because he'd done the same thing before, two weeks before my first visit to the doctor. It immediately hit me: he knew back then. Master Disaster knew I had cancer before the examinations and the tests and the scans made it official. For a split second, I wanted to ask him if it was true.

But I already knew the answer. And it probably wasn't a question he wanted to hear.

When he took his hand away, I could tell he wanted to talk. He was doing that fanning action with his fingers in front of his face, and his legs were bouncing like jackhammers. Must've done it for a good five minutes. Then he gave me a long hug. It was a huge effort because, as you know, he's more of a drive-by hugger. And my fever was through the roof, so touching me couldn't have been much fun. After a while, he let go, leaned back and squeezed his fists together in front of his eyes. He said, "Don't worry, Dad. I'll take good care of Justine."

By the time he opened his hands and put them down in his lap—probably about ten seconds later—I had tears running down my cheeks. He said he would do all the chores he was supposed to do and more. He would quit working his "special job" at Troy's Car Care on Saturday mornings and get a "real job." He would get better at cooking. Learn how to drive. Do handyman stuff around the house, the way I used to. He said he would do something amazing one day so that he and you wouldn't have to worry about anything. He had three ideas for that. Become a stuntman for Jackie Chan. Take the first proper photograph of the Loch Ness Monster and sell it to Yahoo! And warn governments and city councils of earthquakes before they happen and earn reward money. Good ideas like these would *earn lots of cash. He reckoned the two of you could live happily ever after.*

Is it possible that the happiest and saddest moment of your life can be one and the same?

JUSTINE

I'M LYING ON THE BEACH, NAKED, staring at the infinite heavens. Instinctively, I understand three truths:

I am in Crusoe's tale again.

I am myself and not the castaway.

The story ends here.

Am I dead? I know something happened, something sudden and grave. Was it here on the island, within the fog of delusion? Or in the real world, which has no shape or character I can presently invoke? If there is an answer, it likely won't fall out of the clear blue sky above.

I can't move my extremities. I sense they still work—just not at the moment. They're cut off, oblivious to any commands issued from the brain. My only movement is from the neck up. I turn my head to the left. The island is bare, stripped of any and all identity. Every tree, every rock, every bird, every bug...gone. Even the mountains are absent; the cavernous spaces where they once stood are filled with dead air. Nothing remains except the beach and barren ground. I turn my head to the right. A single ship is visible a mile out from shore. It's the rescue vessel, the one that transported the castaway back to England after twenty-eight years off the map. Is it anchored, waiting for me? No. A short observation confirms it is unfastened and on the move. The realization I am being left behind triggers panic. I want to shout out, yell and scream across the water. I want to jump to my feet and sprint into the shallows, waving my arms above my head. I can do neither. I am bound to lay here, mute and motionless, tears streaking the sand, until the ship fades into the horizon.

It should not be happening like this. Mutiny has overrun the story. If I were returning to the homeland, I would be off the island and sailing the high seas. If I am destined to remain in exile—as several men did following Crusoe's departure—then why am I here on my own, unable to speak or move, surrounded by desolation, without a prayer of survival? The answer would appear obvious:

This isn't a dream.

I am dead.

In the instant the thought is confirmed, I hear a sound. Sand scuffing and squelching, quiet at first, then loud, rhythmic. Feet. Bare feet. Leaving imprints on the beach. The sound is directly behind me, in line with my head. I turn left and right, trying to glimpse my companion in death, to no avail. Is it a friend? The captain, volunteering to stay on with the commander? One of the search party, already succumbed to isolation's madness? Is it a foe?

A Moor, perhaps? Or a cannibal? Or is my finder the very source of my former existence—my man, Friday?

The visitor moves to my side, kneels next to me. I turn. The sun is blinding. I blink several times and a face materializes. A young face, yet hard, worn from conflict and subsistence, a childhood endured rather than gifted. A face fashioned from the unforgiving earth.

Xury. He grasps my hand, and the contact revives my sense of touch. Three fingers. Middle, ring, pinkie.

·············●●·············

"ARE YOU SEEING ME?"

I breathe, nod my head. "Yes."

"Positive?"

"Yes."

"How many fingers am I holding up?" Perry holds up two fingers, positions them close to my nose.

"Seven."

"Excellent. You are making good progress, Miss Just Jeans."

My brother flicks his head, squeezes my hand. His eyes are drawn. His nose is red. He's rocking from foot to foot. I look around. The wall to the right is a nest of switches and knobs and lights and cords. A floral curtain separates us from the sighing, grousing creature I can hear in the next bed. A saline drip runs into my wrist.

"How are you feeling?"

I take stock. "Bit groggy. I'm guessing I've got a fair few drugs in me."

"That's correct. I don't need medication, but my sister does."

I laugh, and a steel trap closes over my chest. "Aaaah, bad idea. God, what the hell happened to me?"

"You don't remember getting hurt?"

"Not exactly."

"What do you remember?"

I tell him. In the shower, I pressed my forehead to the tiles and wept. And maybe my sorrow possessed an energy powerful enough to move objects because the shower-curtain rings started to rattle on the bar. Then the little shampoo bottles fell off the shelf. The soap hit the drain hole with a thump. Water spat and gurgled and choked the pipes. Everything shook and shimmied and pulsed like a plucked guitar string. His warning rode the crest of the oncoming seismic waves: *37 percent chance of an 8.2-plus event and a 10 to 15 percent chance of a 9.0-plus event… sometime in the next fifty years…*

The earth couldn't wait fifty years; it figured now to be as good a time as any, lives were due for a shake-up.

I tried to shout out to you as the rumble grew. I tried to yell at the top of my lungs. I went to step out and slipped. My feet had no purchase. The ground had given way. I fell. And Hell's own pain caught me. By the head. Across the chest.

"Next thing I know, I'm here," I conclude. "There's obviously more to the story."

Perry nods.

"Do you want to fill in the blanks?"

Perry gives three big shakes of the head. "Not me." He releases my hand, begins wiping his palms on his thighs. "I want to pretend someone else rescued you. If it's someone else, it's easier to talk about it."

"You don't have to relive what happened, Pez."

He takes a few deep breaths, whispers the prana-something word Mum taught him. "I think it's important you know what happened, so I want to pretend someone else helped you. If it's someone else, it's easier to talk about it."

I nod as tears kiss the corners of my eyes. No crying. Gritting my teeth, I sit up straight, lift the pillows supporting my back. He needs to see I am focused wholly, absolutely, on him. He begins, and I'm not at all surprised by the hero he chooses to save the day.

·········●·········

"**...THEN A DOCTOR CAME TO SPEAK** to Jackie Chan in the corridor. Dr. Michelle Craig. She apologized for taking a long time; the earthquake meant there were more patients to treat than usual. They had done a second set of scans on Just Jeans's heart and brain—everything appeared okay. There was no evidence of major internal injury or bleeding. No spinal concerns. She had a badly bruised sternum, three broken ribs and a heavy concussion. They'd given her drugs. She would need to stay in ICU for a day or two, then maybe a day in the regular ward. But she would be okay. She would have her fair share of pain to deal with, and a flight back to Australia was out of the question for a time, but she would be fine. Jackie Chan asked Dr. Craig if he could see her. The doctor nodded and said he ought to be her first sight upon waking.

"He walked into her room. He placed the seismometer on the bedside table. He waited. As the minutes ticked by, he told her what to expect when she woke up:

"*Just Jeans, it's a good thing I am not moving to Fair Go and we are staying together. You need a caregiver. Not just for your recovery, but for the rest of your life. The earth won't stop—at any time it can shake you up, throw you down and leave you for dead. I wish it wasn't unstable and unpredictable, but that's how the world is. So, someone has to look out for all of us. Someone has to look out for you. Someone who knows you and loves you. Someone brave and strong. Someone who practices first aid. Someone excellent at telling jokes. Someone special.*

"Jackie Chan let her know he would always be there for her. No lie."

············•●•············

I WANT TO DO EVERYTHING in this moment. I want to climb out of bed, hold my brother and never let go. I want to dam the tears streaming down my face. I want to find words to sum up my boundless gratitude. I can't do any of it. I can only hope I'm not dreaming again.

"There are two more things you need to know," continues Perry, avoiding eye contact. "I don't need to pretend for these—I will talk about them as myself. The first is this: Marc is on his way over here."

A small mortar detonates in my chest. I wipe my cheeks with a tissue.

"Once I knew you would be okay, I phoned him. He saw a story about the quake posted on the website for *The Australian*. He said he didn't want to call you because you wanted nothing to do with him—"

"I was an idiot."

"He said he was too. He called himself many bad names, actually. Then he got very upset when I told him what had happened to you. He said every fiber of his being wanted to jump on a plane and come over and see you and take care of you. But he wasn't going to do it."

"How come?"

"He said he respects you too much and he can still learn some things, despite having been to university. He also said he believed you were in good hands."

"I am. So, he wasn't coming…but now he is?"

"I told him when an earthquake happens, people need as much help as possible. We could use *his* help, if he could give it. I felt this was appropriate to say because you had written *Call Marc and apologize* on your to-do list. He took a long time to convince—almost twenty minutes. He didn't want to screw everything up and make you mad again." Perry forms a fist with his right hand, squeezes it till the knuckles blanch. "I hope you're not mad at me."

"Mad? You're kidding, right?"

"No."

"I am *not* mad at you, Pez. Cross my heart and hope to die."

Perry uncurls his fist and bounces the butt of his palm against his forehead. "That is a very bad joke. Now, the second thing—"

"Is it Mum?"

"Yes. She is here. I phoned her on the way to the hospital and left a message that she needed to be here. She came."

"Where is she?"

"She's in the waiting room. She said she'd see you whenever you were ready."

"She's been waiting a while."

"Yes. She's hurt."

"What?"

"She was injured. In the earthquake."

Another thorn lodges in my chest. "Is she okay?"

Perry tips his hand back and forth. "She was brought to the hospital by a neighbor. She was dizzy and nauseous for a while. Her face is the worst. She has cuts, maybe a broken nose."

"Has a doctor seen her?"

"I don't believe so. She refused, said she didn't want help. She said there were other people who needed treatment more than her."

I suck in as much breath as my ruined ribs will allow. Dad's words descend like open parachutes: *Love is reliable. You can depend on it.*

Perry coughs into his hand. "I think Mum should come in now, yes?"

I nod. He turns, takes three steps, pauses. He hunches his shoulders and wheels around to face me once more.

"I asked Mum if you and I and Marc could stay at her house until you are well again and we can get another flight back to Brisbane. It seemed like a logical solution."

"What did she say?"

"She said *of course* and then she cried. She said we will always be welcome at the Ne'er Go residence. Ne'er...Do you know what that means?"

"It's an abbreviation of *never*."

He thinks it over for a few seconds, then breaks into a smile. "Ne'er Go instead of Fair Go—it's a joke!"

"It is, sort of. We'll work with her, help her be better."

"Yes," says Perry, clapping his hands. "We will help her be better."

·········●··········

I'M DONE NOW. I NEED TO REST.

Our trip is done too. We've arrived at...well, here. In a few short moments, brother and mother will stand at the foot of my hospital bed. Three remnants of the Richter family: separated but together, injured but healed, directionless but moving on. Spared by Fate. And all of it just as we'd planned.

Yeah, totally.

I let my head fall to the right. The seismometer sits watch on the bedside table. With the last threads of energy in my body, I want to reach out and touch it, tap into its secrets. What information does it hold? What will it reveal as the dawn becomes the day? Only Master Disaster knows—or, at least, retains the capacity to know. That's as it should be. The future is best kept in his hands. He is quite capable.

Floating now.

Floating toward sleep.

Toward night.

In the past, I scoured the dark for revelations. No more. Every epiphany I ever sought has been exposed, not by the night sky above my head but by the shifting earth beneath my feet.

I hear footsteps on linoleum. I think it's linoleum. Maybe it's sand. The door creaks open and the footsteps close in. I smell the print of a new book, taste cigarette smoke. I can't see, though. Can't focus. Sleep is taking me away, but it's okay. I know they're present.

Love is reliable.

Everything is still.

...........●...........

1 October 2008

This is the last entry, Justine. We're still a few weeks away from your birthday, but I want to give you this journal first thing in the morning. Actually, I <u>need</u> to give you this first thing in the morning. I'm not feeling too good, Jus. Stuff is slipping away—fast. Reckon I'll be knockin' on the pearly gates sooner rather than later. I'm ready. I hope you are, too. I think you are.

There are two things I want you to know. The first is that I love you and Perry more than I can say or write or even breathe with these jiggered lungs of mine. I loved you, Jus, from the second you were born. From the moment the nurse put you into my arms and you looked up at my ugly mug with those searching eyes. And nothing's changed since. That's the way it's stayed. If any father has loved his kids more during his time on this earth, then I tip my hat to him.

The second thing is about your brother. We've talked a lot and I know you said you'd take care of him. And I've got no doubt in this world and the next that you will. To me, Jus, your word is as solid as steel. But here's the thing: I want you to take care of yourself too. I want you to find the middle ground, where you're not just keeping him happy but you're creating some happiness of your own. That was the way I tried to be over the years. I hope that comes through when you read this journal. Perry was never a chore to me. Master Disaster was never a weight on my shoulders. I never felt I was denied anything because he was my son. I had it good. I had it bloody good.

Life is short, my little tree frog. Make it your only complaint when all is said and done.

PERRY

IN 1989 AUSTRALIANS GAVE MONEY and food and furniture and toys and even themselves to rebuild the devastated city of Newcastle. The governments helped too—for every dollar that was donated, they gave one as well. Within a month, 14,000 people had received assistance. Within nine months, almost $4.5 million had been distributed to the victims. Following the 2004 Indian Ocean catastrophe, the public in the United Kingdom responded with £330 million (almost US$600 million); the amount averaged out to be around £5.50 (US$10) from every person in the nation. The awful 2008 tragedy of Sichuan Province saw everyday people from all over mainland China dig deep into their pockets at special booths set up in banks, schools and near petrol stations. They also donated blood, their generosity causing long queues in most of the big Chinese cities.

Vancouver is rallying and rebuilding now. Not as much as Newcastle or Aceh or Sichuan, but enough to have the community working together. That includes me—I've been helping to get Mum's home back to normal. There was no major structural damage to the townhouse;

the load-bearing walls were okay, and the foundation slab didn't crack or break. It was mainly the stuff inside the house that didn't fare too well. I was responsible for quite a few of the fixes—clearing the living room floor; shaking out the rug; moving the fridge back into its proper position; putting the pictures back up on the sideboard and the piano; ensuring all the pieces of the shattered mirror in the bathroom were picked up—even the slivers—so no one would cut their feet. Off my own bat, I also made sure all the lightbulbs were working, because I don't like the dark. I was able to complete all these tasks independently.

At this moment, I'm finishing another job, an easy and comforting one, and the last on the long list: car wash. Gray Ford Taurus. It belongs to Mum. Following the quake, her car was covered in dust and particles from the roof (I imagine it looked a bit like the ash of Mount St. Helens). Once everything in the house was rebuilt or replaced or put back pretty much the way it was, I was able to give the car my full attention and washologist expertise.

Now, it's done. I stand back and assess my work. Spotless windows, good body shine, tires look almost new again. The swirling scents of wax and environmentally friendly detergent tease my nose. Given that I didn't have my usual equipment from Troy's, the Taurus has come up quite well. No lie.

I wring out the sponge and empty the black water into a nearby drain. A cool wind whips through the townhouse parking lot, ruffling my damp T-shirt. The leaves of the cherry blossom tree overlooking the complex have changed color again in the last ten days, from orange-red to brown. They're falling, too, creating a scrabbly carpet on the pavement. It's funny—they clung to the tree during the earthquake, but now they're letting go. Mother Nature always decides when the time is right.

Back inside the house, I peel off my T-shirt, drop it in the brand-new washing machine. I stretch my arms, my neck, my back. A yoga routine would be good to help my out-of-practice carwashing muscles recover. Entering the living room, I figure Extrasensory Leonie must've read my mind. She's in the center of the room, performing *Garudasana*, Eagle pose. The mat under her feet—I chose it. It wasn't handmade in an ashram. It cost thirty bucks at Open Space in the village. I got one for myself too.

Looking over the open space remaining here in the room, I don't think there's enough for me to pose along with Mum. I don't want to crowd Marc—he's standing on the stepladder, attaching L-brackets to the top of the bookshelf. Just Jeans is reading *The Apprenticeship of Duddy Kravitz* in the armchair, reclining with the footrest out; maintaining this position is crucial because she still needs to limit the strain on her chest. Oh well—no yoga for me just yet. There'll be plenty of time later tonight. And in the ten days before Jus and Marc and I fly back to Brisbane. And in the two or so months before Mum arrives. We can do routines together using Skype.

I sit down at the dining table and watch the quiet scene, like a seismologist carefully considering the data at his disposal. Even though the trio is busy doing their own thing, they're also comfortable sharing this space. Some quality time in the Ne'er Go residence has brought them closer together in more places than the living room. They don't notice me watching them—I like that, the chance to observe without conversation or questions. And what do I see? I see a happy ending, like *The Forbidden Kingdom* final scenes when Jason returns home after ending the Jade Warlord's reign of terror. Of course, it's not really the end—Jackie Chan's blooper reels during the credits of his films show there is always more to the story. Someday, this calm and peaceful sight before my eyes will be a nice memory in the backs of all our minds. Things will get shaken up again, broken into pieces, and we will need to put it all back together the best we can. And we will, because although we can't rely on a stable, predictable Earth in the years to come, we can rely on each other.

That is the future.

That is today.

ACKNOWLEDGMENTS

As Perry says, *We can't live in a world of one*, and that's particularly true for an author writing a novel. I'd like to sincerely thank the following people for helping me bring this story together: my beautiful wife, Wend; my twins; the Brothers Groth; Mum and Dad; the Fraser Clan; my agents, Tara Wynne and John Pearce; Zoe Walton, Catriona Murdie and the Random House team; Ruth Linka, Sarah Harvey and Jen Cameron at Orca Book Publishers; Claire Kamber; the BCLC Bandwagon; "Legend Hunter" Bill Steciuk; Daniel Defoe; and the great man himself, Jackie Chan.

I couldn't have done it without you. No lie.

ABOUT THE AUTHOR

Originally from Brisbane, Australia, Darren Groth now lives in Vancouver, British Columbia, with his Canadian wife and thirteen-year-old twins. His books have been published on both sides of the Pacific and include *Kindling* and *Most Valuable Potential*, which was short-listed for the Queensland Premier's Literary Awards—Young Adult Book Award. The 2014 Australian edition of *Are You Seeing Me?* was recently selected a 2014 Book of the Year by Booktopia and a 2015 Outstanding Book for the International Board on Books for Young People (IBBY) collection.

Darren has appeared at numerous literary events, including the Byron Bay Writers Festival and Brisbane Writers Festival. He has been a guest speaker, workshop and master-class facilitator and writer-in-residence for literary organizations, writing groups, schools and libraries, and has written articles for publications including *The Courier-Mail*, *Writing Queensland* and *Mamamia*. For more information, visit www.darrengroth.com.